DEAD DICK

R. Scott Bolton

Copyright 2021 by R. Scott Bolton
ISBN: 978-0-9997962-3-8

A Rough Edge Studios Production
www.roughedgestudios.com

This book is dedicated to my grandmother, Dorothy Farmer. We call her Granny. When I was a little boy, she would sit with me in front of the TV and we would watch monster movies together. To this day, I remember sitting in her living room and watching my favorite monster, *The Creature from the Black Lagoon,* on that tiny black-and-white screen. So, if my mind seems a little warped, now you know who to blame.

As always, thanks to my ever-vigilant Quality Control Team. The readers listed below offered opinions and corrections that helped form the completed work, and I can never thank them enough for their input. But I'll try: Thanks to Shelley Bolton, Josh Bolton, Doug Bolton, Sue Bolton, John DeRuvo, Jeff Rogers, Steve Snider and Keith Guyotte.

Also, a special shout-out to the National Novel Writing Month non-profit organization. Each November, they challenge their participants to write a novel in thirty days. I started in 2013 and have completed the first draft of a novel every year since. DEAD DICK was the second book I completed under their program. I heartily recommend NaNoWriMo to anyone who is considering writing a novel, screenplay, stage play or whatever. NaNoWriMo helps keep you focused. Check them out and feel free to donate: www.nanowrimo.org.

CHAPTER ONE — June 2, 1954

Not for the first time in his life, Richard Keane thought, *I am on the wrong side of this business.*

He palmed the wide steering wheel of his sky blue 1951 Plymouth Cambridge and turned into the short driveway leading to 1511 Sunset Boulevard. The driveway was only about five feet deeper than the sidewalk and grass strip that separated the property from the street, and Keane brought the Cambridge to a squeaking stop at the black wrought iron gate that blocked his way. He reached out of the driver's side window and punched the tip of his finger against the button set below a speaker box impaled on a post there. A hand-written sign, Scotch-taped to the post, read, "Please push and state your business."

Keane waited impatiently for a response from whoever was on the other side of the speaker line inside the massive home hidden behind the gate. Experience told him there would be no reply. These types of automated gate entrances only worked ten or twenty percent of the time, a fact he had proven himself from years of working in upper class Los Angeles, and he knew the odds were against him. As another thirty seconds passed, Keane shook his head in frustration. *Swell*, he thought. *Probably have to go back to the office and call them again.*

No sooner had that thought crossed his mind than the speaker box beeped and a tinny voice buzzed, "State your name and business." Keane frowned. *Oops*, he thought, *forgot that part. Should have pushed the switch* and *stated my business.*

"Richard Keane," he said in a loud, clear voice. "I have an appointment with Mr. Mukasa."

There was another lengthy delay and Keane was just about to repeat himself when the disembodied voice droned, "Please enter," and, with a shuddering mechanical clanking, the wrought iron gate slowly began to swing open.

"Thanks," Keane muttered, wondering if the person on the other end could still hear him or had already disconnected. He put the Cambridge into gear and drove slowly onto the property.

The long and twisting cement driveway that led to the house meandered like a flat white snake and Keane followed it carefully and slowly, concerned that another vehicle might come racing toward him from the opposite direction. There wasn't enough room on the small lane for two cars to pass and, if there wasn't an accident, at the very least someone would have to back up. There were big round mirrors stuck in the ground like giant lollipops, ostensibly for drivers to see around the hairpin corners but, as far as Keane could tell, they all faced bad angles and reflected only images of the thick shrubbery surrounding the driveway.

Keane felt as though he were moving through a tunnel of foliage. Huge trees lined each side of the drive, their thick aged trunks reaching up and opening into multitudinous branches that hung heavy with bright green leaves. Between each tree trunk was a wall of shrubbery, so thick and lush that he could see only brief swatches of the brick wall behind it.

It was the second day of June. The Southern California summer was in full swing and the trees were soaking up the blazing sun like alligator lizards basking on the hot afternoon sidewalk.

After what seemed an impossibly long drive (*How far back* is *this house from the Boulevard?* Keane wondered) the shrubbery faded away and the low brick wall, maybe five or six feet tall, took over. The wall was divided into ten-foot sections and, at the end of each section, a solid brick column stood, giving the wall strength and style. Placed atop each column was a bigger-than-life marble statue, the likes of which Keane remembered seeing at the Los Angeles County Museum of Art. Topless, full-bodied women hid their presumably exposed pudendum with seashells the size of dinner plates. Naked men, their stone penises dangling in unabashed repose, gripped empty drinking vessels, harps or arrows at their sides. Cherubic children sat atop stone pillars, reaching to the sky, arching their backs in childish pleasure. And there was even one statue of fellow citizens locked in what appeared to be an Olympian wrestling match, one man above grappling with another below, the furor of their contest apparent in the style and cut of their stone faces.

Keane slowed the Cambridge in order to admire the statuary. He was no scholar of Roman mythology or ancient art but he could see that these weren't your usual lawn jockeys. While they may not have been the original statues that stood in Roman courtyards, they were very high quality and thus very expensive replicas and therefore worth a closer look.

Suddenly, Keane braked the car to a halt and peered over the top of his black-rimmed Ray-Ban sunglasses. He squinted at the statue of an armored Roman centurion on the column before him, spear held in its left hand, shield hanging loosely by its hip. Was that the early afternoon sunlight playing a trick on his eyes? Or was the hair beneath its crested helmet painted a glossy black?

It wasn't the sunlight or the shadows, Keane realized after a moment, but an actual addition to the classic statue. Someone had taken the time to give the statue a touch of realism with a paint brush and some black paint. He glanced around at the other statues and realized there had been other enhancements as well. A pair of eyebrows

5

painted here, a pair of lips reddened there. One nude male statue sported a lipstick kiss on its right cheek.

Keane shook his head. *Why do I always get the crazy ones?* he thought, remembering the day he'd received the phone call that had brought him here.

CHAPTER TWO — May 30, 1954

It had been only a few days ago, just an hour before noon, on the second to last day of May. Keane sat in his West Los Angeles office, staring out at the palm trees that lined Sunset Boulevard on both sides. The Spartan use of space inside had impressed many a visitor. There was only the modest wooden desk, a high-backed leather chair behind it, two fabric upholstered guest chairs in front of the desk and a wooden coat rack standing tall in one corner. There was no artwork on the dull yellow walls but they bore hundreds of tiny pinholes made by hundreds of Saf-T-Head thumbtacks. During an investigation, Keane often had those walls layered with photos, notes and other types of evidence.

On the desktop was only a small desk fan, its blades spinning breathlessly, an old Royal typewriter that seemed cast completely out of solid iron, a Biff's coffee cup containing pens and pencils that jutted up proudly like arrows in a quiver, and a telephone, painfully silent.

Stenciled across the dappled glass of the window that made up the top half of the office door, the words "Richard Keane, Private Investigator," boldly stated the name and occupation of the tenant inside.

Keane frowned down at the telephone. It hadn't rung in a week and the last few cases he'd taken had been quick, easy and low paying: A wife wanted her husband followed because she was sure he'd been cheating on her (he wasn't); An elderly couple asked him to find their lost daughter, who had disappeared nearly a month before (Keane found her in a gypsy camp where she had taken up with a handsome and swift-talking pickpocket); A local attorney had asked him to deliver a summons to a witness who was proving difficult to locate (Keane had delivered the summons to the target at the Stan's Drive-In Coffee Shop just down the road during lunch hour).

Quick. Easy. Low paying. The total balance remaining from those three services according to his checkbook? $57. Barely enough to cover the rent.

Keane shook his head. A cheeseburger from Stan's sounded pretty good right now. Too bad his bank account was nearly empty and his wallet contained just two single dollar bills.

Regrettably, there was nothing more he could do than wait. So, he kicked off his shoes, leaned back in his creaky office chair, put his face in the bowl of his fedora and settled in for a quick nap. That's when the inevitable happened: The phone on his desk rang. Despite being in a nearly prone position, Keane was able to answer it on the second ring.

"Richard Keane," he said. "Private Investigator."

"Mr. Keane," said a low, rumbling voice. Keane thought the accent sounded Middle Eastern. "I understand you are a private detective."

"I am," Keane said. *Didn't I just say that?*

"Then I am in need of your services," said the voice. "I understand you are the best."

"So I've been told," Keane replied, thinking he'd never been told anything like that. "What can I help you with?"

"My name is Arnold Mukasa. Perhaps you have heard of me?"

Keane nodded but said nothing. He had indeed heard of Arnold Mukasa. Mukasa's life was one of those inspiring stories that could only have taken place in Hollywood. The Mukasa family was of Ugandan descent and had come to America in the early 1920s to try to find a better life. Things were tough at first, as they were for many immigrants at that time. Arnold, only 14 years old, had often gone to bed hungry as his father struggled to find work in construction, in the fields or any other type of manual labor, even if for only a day at a time. Arnold did what he could to help: Ran errands for neighbors, carried groceries for elderly shoppers, sold newspapers during big news days when the papers were far more plentiful and in higher demand. There was never enough for his family to live comfortably, but it was enough to keep them alive.

And then, at the age of 17, Arnold had almost literally stumbled into William Farrell. Returning home very late from a last minute grocery delivery for an elderly neighbor—via an alley that was a shortcut to his home—Arnold found Farrell passed out, face up, in the gutter behind a neighborhood bar called "The Drink." Arnold was shocked to find the man unconscious on the pavement and horrified to discover that he appeared to be choking on his own vomit. Thinking quickly, Arnold rolled Farrell over onto his side and let the puke drain out, feeling a wave of relief when the man started taking deep, ragged breaths. Afraid of what would happen if he left him alone, Arnold stayed at his side until the drunk awoke nearly three hours later. Arnold all but carried Farrell back to the man's nearby home where he helped Farrell shower and put on fresh clothing.

It wasn't until they were inside Farrell's home that Arnold realized who he had rescued. Adorning the walls inside were layers of movie posters, flyers and programs bearing the man's name, and Arnold suddenly remembered he had seen that name before on the big screen at the local movie theater. Farrell was a legendary entertainment producer. Stage. Film. And making his way into the burgeoning world of television.

The story went on to say that when Farrell awakened the next morning (with the mother of all hangovers pounding at his skull) he was surprised and grateful to find Arnold still sitting near his bedside, waiting patiently and anxiously. Touched and genuinely thankful for the boy's help and concern, Farrell immediately hired Arnold as his driver and personal assistant.

That simple job began the swing that led Arnold Mukasa from street urchin to chauffeur to movie producer. In fact, Arnold Mukasa was now one of the biggest producers of motion pictures in the world. Bigger, even, than his mentor, William Farrell.

So, of course, Richard Keane knew of Arnold Mukasa. Everyone, especially those in Los Angeles, knew the man's name. But Keane thought it better, for the moment, to pretend otherwise. "Doesn't ring a bell," he said.

"It isn't important who I am," Mukasa said with complete nonchalance. Keane thought that, if the man was disturbed by Keane's ignorance, he was hiding it brilliantly. "I am a film producer and a man with considerable wealth. I wish to engage your services in the kidnapping of my daughter."

Keane knew about that as well. There had been little else in the newspapers for the past few days other than the story about the kidnapping of the wealthy film producer's daughter.

"I'm sorry to hear that," Keane said, continuing the charade. "When was she kidnapped?"

"Eight days ago," Mukasa told him and Keane heard his voice catch in his throat. "She was found dead two days ago in a field near the beach at Point Dume. She had been strangled."

"My deepest condolences, sir," Keane said solemnly. "And the police have no leads?"

"The police have nothing to go on whatsoever. They will continue their investigation, of course, but I am not confident of their success."

"I understand," Keane said. "It never hurts to have someone else on your side. Would you like to come down to my office, sign some papers, discuss a fee?"

"I'd rather you came to my home, Mr. Keane," said Mukasa. "As you might imagine, my family is in quite a state of distress and we have a great deal of mourning to do. I would be more comfortable, if you don't mind, if you came to me."

"Of course," Keane said. "I understand completely. What is the address please?"

Mukasa gave him the address and Keane noted without surprise that it was in one of the richest neighborhoods in Hollywood, perhaps in the world. A series of mansions and sprawling estates that only the richest and most famous could afford to call home.

"When can you be here?" Mukasa asked.

"Tomorrow morning, 8:00am.," Keane said.

"Let's make it tomorrow afternoon," Mukasa suggested. "Say 2:00pm?"

"That will work," Keane said. "Again, I am truly sorry for your loss, Mr. Mukasa."

"I look forward to meeting you, Mr. Keane."

And the line went dead.

CHAPTER THREE — June 2, 1954

Keane took the final corner on the long, snake-like drive and turned into a circular driveway shaped like a lasso. One way in, same way out. A gleaming black Cadillac Fleetwood limousine reposed there, its repetitious route apparent from the tire grooves worn in the gravel that trailed behind its rear tires. Directly across from the car rose an enormous white-columned home, massive by any standard, with multiple windows on both the first and second floors and a huge single door set between two massive columns that towered like giant bookends on each side. Keane was first shocked and then resigned to see that someone had painted the front door and window frames a bright pink. *Not pink, of course*, Keane thought, *Probably fuchsia or some other fancy word for pink.* He sighed. *No accounting for taste.*

He brought the Cambridge to a halt and killed the engine. Removing the keys from the ignition, he snatched his briefcase off the passenger seat and stepped out. As he came around the front of the car, the pink door of the mansion opened and a gaunt man, his papery flesh white almost to the point of translucence, stepped onto the front porch and bowed a stiff greeting.

"Mr. Keane, I presume?" he asked in a reedy but refined voice.

"Yes."

"I am Charles, Mr. Mukasa's manservant. Would you follow me, please?"

"Of course."

Charles turned on his heel and re-entered the home. Keane followed him obediently.

Inside, Keane was unsurprised, but nonetheless impressed, by the home's regal interior. He stepped into the foyer and took in his surroundings as Charles closed the door behind him. Directly in front of him a marble staircase climbed up to the second story, splitting off at the top and curling around both sides to the second-floor landing. On each side of the spacious foyer stood more of the Roman statues (*sans* painted hair, Keane noted) and huge marble vases from which sprung various tropical-looking bushes and vines, lush and full. The floor beneath his feet was also marble and gleamed with the evidence that someone took great care to keep it maintained.

"Please wait here for a moment," Charles said. "I will see if Mr. Mukasa is ready to greet you. May I take your bag?"

"No, thank you," Keane said.

"I will only be a moment," Charles told him.

As Charles disappeared down a hallway, Keane continued to admire the Mukasa home. Located near the door was a marble umbrella bin, three hooked umbrella handles poking out of it. *Not going to need those for a while*, Keane thought, thinking of the L.A. summer heat still to come. To the left of the staircase was a recessed alcove inside of which was a polished wooden table bearing two immense vases overflowing with bright, fresh, colorful flowers.

Above the table hung a large lively portrait of an obviously dynamic young girl, her instantly infectious smile as bright as the sun, her blonde hair tumbling around her face playfully. Keane felt his heart warm at the girl's obvious love of life and the way that her pure joy had been perfectly captured by the artist's brush. He couldn't resist returning her smile, as though it were not a mere portrait but that rather the girl was there, in the flesh.

"Yes, she had that effect on people," said a voice behind him. Keane turned and found a small man approaching him. He wore a shiny silk smoking jacket and what appeared to be matching pajama bottoms. Keane was struck by the dark circles under the man's eyes and his wild, unruly hair. He looked as though he hadn't slept in days, seemed unhealthy. Fragile.

"She brought happiness to everyone she met," Arnold Mukasa said. "That was my Kimmy."

Keane glanced once more at the portrait of Mukasa's late daughter and extended his hand. "Richard Keane," he said, as they shook.

"Yes, and I am Arnold Mukasa. Please forgive my appearance. It has been a troubling past few days."

"I understand, sir," Keane said. "And, again, I am very sorry for your loss."

"Have you been following the story in the newspapers, Mr. Keane?"

"I confess that I have," Keane admitted. "When you called, I couldn't be sure it wasn't some kind of joke, so I pretended not to know the name. Sorry for the ruse."

"Not at all, Mr. Keane. In fact, that sounds very wise. I feel as though I have found the right gentleman. Will you follow me to the study, please?"

"Of course."

"May Charles get you something to drink? Coffee, perhaps? Tea?"

"A glass of water would be fine."

"Of course. Charles?"

"Right away, sir," Charles chimed and was off in a flash.

Keane followed Mukasa through a hallway—lined, like the foyer, with marble tables and vases of colorful flowers—to a smaller but equally glorious room near the left side of the home. This room appeared to have been designed more for comfort, Keane observed, eyeing the padded chairs lining one wall and an overstuffed sofa planted along another. A massive mahogany desk commanded the middle of the room, an unnecessarily giant leather chair resting behind it. Mukasa padded over and took the giant leather chair, all but disappearing into it, and indicated that Keane should sit in one of the two chairs directly before him. Keane waited until Mukasa was completely seated and then took his place in the chair on the left, leaving his briefcase on the lush carpet beneath him.

"As we discussed during our telephone conversation yesterday," Mukasa said after a moment. "And as you have read in the newspapers, my daughter was taken eight days ago, and we have received no demand, no note or any other type of contact from the kidnappers."

Keane nodded.

"And she was found dead two days ago on a beach near Point Dume."

"Yes," Keane said. "Again, my condolences."

"What does this tell you?"

"It would seem to me," Keane said, "And I'm sorry to be blunt, Mr. Mukasa, but it seems to me that kidnapping was never really the intended action."

Mukasa steepled his fingers. "Go on."

"Kidnappers do what they do for a reason," Keane said. "Money. They want ransom. Kidnappers take someone and then contact their loved ones, demanding payment for their safe return. But you never received any type of communication from the kidnappers, is that right?"

Mukasa nodded grimly.

"Which tells me," Keane continued. "That kidnapping was never their goal. I'm sorry, Mr. Mukasa, but I think your daughter was taken for more nefarious reasons."

"They took her to kill her?" Mukasa asked breathlessly.

"Perhaps," Keane said. "But there are other possibilities as well. There are a lot of sick people out there, Mr. Mukasa. Perverts, child pornographers, drug abusers, child traffickers. Again, I apologize for being blunt. The fact that she was strangled also discounts kidnapping and indicates a crime of some sick passion."

Keane was alarmed to see Mukasa's already pale features growing even more so. "Of course," he continued, "It is possible that your daughter may indeed have been taken for ransom purposes and then something went awry. Until we find out who did this, we may never know."

"Do you think you can find them?" Mukasa said. "The ones who did this?"

Keane took a deep breath. "I'll be honest, sir. I don't know. The police have only had a week or so to investigate so it's really not surprising that they haven't come up with any leads. And their investigation changed from a kidnapping investigation to a murder investigation just a couple of days ago."

Charles re-entered the study and placed a tall glass of water on the desk in front of Keane. Ice tinkled against the fine crystal glass. He stepped around the table and set a cup of steaming tea in front of Mukasa.

"Thank you, Charles," Mukasa whispered. Charles left the room. Mukasa looked directly into Keane's eyes. "So, you don't think you can do any more than the police?"

"That's not what I'm saying," Keane said quickly. "I'm just saying they may not have had enough time to do a proper investigation. But I don't want to give you false hope. I'm not going to promise that I can find the persons responsible for what happened to your daughter. But I will do my damnedest to do so."

Mukasa fell silent a moment and Keane decided it was best to let the man think. He couldn't imagine what it was like to be in Mukasa's position. To lose a daughter, a young girl, the light of your life. The pain would be unbearable and the desire to do something, anything, would be overwhelming.

And then he thought about Kimmy Mukasa's last few days. She would have been terrified to be taken by strangers, probably treated more roughly than she'd ever been treated in her entire pampered life. They had probably kept her somewhere dark and hidden, perhaps cold and miserable or, in this weather, unbearably hot and close. He thought of her portrait in the hallway, that heart-warming bright smile, the eyes full of wonder and curiosity. And he thought of those eyes in wide-open terror as the life was squeezed out of her and he felt his chest go tight with anger and the desire for revenge.

"Mr. Keane, there is someone I would like you to meet," Mukasa said suddenly. "Please excuse me for just a few moments."

"Of course, sir."

Keane took another sip of his water and sat back in his chair as Mukasa stepped out of the room. *Poor man*, Keane thought. He had everything, had worked hard to earn it all, only to have his life shattered by the kidnapping and death of his only daughter. Keane couldn't begin to imagine the pain of that. And what about Kimmy? A young girl, in love with life, her light taken and extinguished in such a horrible way. Los Angeles was a shitty town sometimes, Keane thought, and sometimes this is a shitty world. He felt a fierce yearning to find the people who had done this and to bring them to justice.

Or, better yet, to put them out of their misery.

The door opened again and Mukasa returned with his guest in tow. Keane took one look at the man and his entire attitude changed. Suddenly, he was no longer sure of anything.

CHAPTER FOUR — June 2, 1954

"This is my employee and close friend, Peter Griswald," Mukasa said, indicating the man by his side. "I'm sure you've seen him at the pictures."

Indeed, Keane had. Griswald was a famous Hollywood personality whose segments often appeared in newsreels before feature films. He claimed to be a psychic and a precognitive. Despite the fact he was almost always wrong, his eerie style and flamboyant personality had made him a star. His once-a-month séances were a highlight of the Hollywood party scene. Keane, of course, had never been but had heard stories of the strange ceremonies and the wild parties that followed them. Keane didn't buy any supernatural shtick—Griswald's or anybody else's for that matter—and he instantly distrusted anybody who said they did.

"Mr. Keane, a pleasure," said Griswald, in a voice that was too close to Bela Lugosi's for Keane's liking, and held out his hand.

Keane stood and took it, was somewhat disgusted by the cold, clammy grip, but was able to mumble, "Pleasure," before taking his seat once again.

"Mr. Keane," Mukasa said, as he took his place behind the mahogany desk and motioned Griswald to the chair beside Keane. "Do you believe in the afterlife?"

Alarm bells went off in Keane's head. The conversation had taken exactly the turn he was afraid it would when Griswald walked into the office. A straight-forward catch-the-kidnappers/killers case had suddenly become infested with a desperate and ludicrous discussion of what happens after we die. Keane wasn't happy at all.

"I'm sorry, that was a loaded question," Mukasa said, apparently sensing Keane's hesitation. "Allow me to re-phrase that. Do you believe the living can communicate with the dead?"

From bad to worse, Keane thought. He considered just getting up and walking out right then but the memory of the two lonely dollar bills in his wallet made him decide to stay. *Maybe*, he hoped, *this will lead back to something useful.* Still, he decided to be frank.

"I do not," he said. "When you're dead, you're dead."

Mukasa gave him a startled look. "Really? Then how do you explain ghosts?"

"I don't," Keane replied. "I've never seen one and I don't personally know anyone who's seen one."

"I've seen one," Griswald said.

"Of course you have," Keane said.

Griswald looked briefly hurt but then the hurt turned to anger. He raised his finger in a "Here, now!" gesture but was cut off by Mukasa.

"We're not here to argue philosophy or theology, gentlemen," Mukasa said. "It is not necessary for the three of us to agree on something in order to proceed."

"Then let's get to the point," Keane said. "What is it exactly that you want of me?"

"I want you to find my daughter's killers."

"Then let's discuss my fees and I'll be on my way," Keane said. "The sooner I can get on the trail, the better."

"There is no reason to discuss your fees, Mr. Keane. As you are aware, I can certainly afford them." Mukasa sat back in his chair and steepled his fingers. "But there is much else for us to discuss before we begin."

Keane didn't like the way Griswald's eyes seemed to glaze over when Mukasa talked about money. But, to be honest, he wasn't sure his eyes weren't glazing over, too. "Very well," he said. "I'm listening."

"You may not believe that one can communicate with the dead, Mr. Keane, but my friend here, Mr. Griswald, not only believes it, he claims that he has done it."

Keane gave Griswald a look that would wither sting weeds. Griswald merely smiled smugly back at him.

"In fact, Mr. Keane, Griswald here claims that he has actually heard from my daughter. That she asks I not worry about her; that I go on with my life and try to forget her which, of course, is impossible."

"Of course," Keane said.

"Mr. Griswald has, at my bidding, asked my daughter about her captors, about her killers. She has remained silent. Mr. Griswald believes that this is because she does not want me to come to harm, either physically or through the law, by attempting to locate the kidnappers and murderers and bring them to justice."

"Is that what you want to do?" Keane asked. "Bring them to justice?"

"Of course not," Mukasa said quickly. "I want them dead. I want the people responsible for the death of my daughter to be drawn and quartered in a public forum. I want them to suffer, Mr. Keane, I want them to feel pain as they've never known."

He brought his hand down on the mahogany desk so hard that Griswald flinched and Keane had to grab his water glass to prevent it from spilling over.

"I know exactly what you mean," Keane said levelly.

"At least we agree on that point," Mukasa said. He took a deep breath, a sip of his tea (Keane thought he could smell the leathery scent of scotch emanating from the cup) and sat back in his chair again. "But I cannot bring that pain to them unless I can find them. I have no faith in the LAPD. The problem seems to be, Mr. Keane, that only my daughter knows who is responsible for her death."

"And how do you know that?" Keane asked.

"Because that's what she told Mr. Griswald," Mukasa said. "When he asked her about her kidnap and murder, she told him there were no witnesses."

Keane shook his head and started to speak. Mukasa held up a hand. "Please, Mr. Keane, allow me to finish. You're on my payroll as of now. Please do not interrupt me again."

"I haven't agreed …"

"There is no need for formalities, Mr. Keane. We both know of your current financial status. You'll take the job."

Keane, surprised but not, shrugged his shoulders and leaned back.

"When Mr. Griswald last spoke to my daughter, during a recent séance at his home, she told him there were no witnesses to either the kidnapping or the murder. She told him that the only people who knew the perpetrators were, in fact, the guilty. And she refused to give him any further information regarding their names or whereabouts."

Keane wanted nothing more than to stand up, punch Griswald hard in the mouth, and leave this house now. But he felt badly for Mukasa's loss and for his desperation to trust in a so-called psychic. He decided to let Mukasa have his say and then politely turn down the job. Meanwhile, Mukasa continued.

"I have asked Mr. Griswald to try to contact someone else in the other world, to see if perhaps there is another there with more information. Someone who has already passed and may know what my daughter knows. His efforts, however, have proved fruitless."

Griswald leaned forward and said in his drunken Dracula voice, "I have done all I can."

"I'm sure," Keane replied acidly.

The study door opened and yet another man entered. Keane identified him instantly as a bodyguard or some other form of muscle. He was big, but Keane quickly ascertained he was no threat. Apparently, Mukasa wasn't about to let anybody leave until he had his say and now he had his muscle blocking the door. Regardless, Keane wasn't worried about walking out of here, bodyguard or not.

"And so it has come to this," Mukasa said. "My daughter has been murdered at the hands of obscene thugs and no one seems to have any notion as to who or why or how. There are no leads, there are no answers and yet my daughter lies in the morgue, her throat ruined by a killer's hands and her heart forever still."

He focused his eyes on Keane. "As you no doubt have guessed, Mr. Keane, I am a desperate man. I have allowed the police the time and opportunity to do their job …"

"I don't think you've allowed them enough time," Keane said.

Mukasa paused at the interruption but then continued. "I have turned to a friend who claims he can speak to the dead, and he has offered me no solace."

Griswald tried to speak, but Mukasa held up a quieting hand.

"And so I have decided this. If no one in this world can help me find the monsters who killed my daughter, then someone in the other world, the afterlife, will find them for me."

Keane's brow wrinkled in confusion. He looked at Griswald, who appeared to be just as puzzled. "But you said you tried to contact others in the afterlife," Keane said, disliking the way the words felt in his mouth. "And had no luck."

"Precisely," Mukasa said. "Which is why, Mr. Keane, I'm sending you."

Keane heard the cocking of the pistol, saw the sudden horror flash across Griswald's face, and then there was a blast and instantly nothing as Mukasa's muscle man shot Keane point blank in the side of the head.

CHAPTER FIVE — June 4, 2015

Dennis Harvey sat in the bar at the Holiday Inn in Tucson, Arizona and mused about how much he loved going on sales trips. He loved the freedom of being on his own; he loved the silence in his hotel room. He relished eating at a different restaurant each night and he loved the cool quietness of a hotel bar on a weeknight. And he truly enjoyed seeing new places and re-visiting old favorites. It was only two or three weeks out of each year but Dennis looked forward to it mightily. It was like a vacation from home life.

Not that he didn't love his wife. In fact, he probably loved her more than most married men who'd woken up to the same woman for nearly twenty years. *And, truth be told*, he thought, *she probably enjoys the quiet time herself. Probably gets enough of me the rest of the year.*

Dennis took another sip of his gin and tonic (something else that he loved that he didn't get enough of at home) and smiled contentedly. Yep. This was the life.

"Haven't seen you here before," said a pleasant voice beside him. Dennis looked over and was surprised to see a woman sitting a couple of stools down. His pulse quickened. Not only did she have a pleasant voice, but she was knock-down, drag-out gorgeous! She had a head full of flowing blonde hair, her skin was the color of cinnamon toast, and the tight white dress she wore contrasted beautifully with the exquisitely exposed flesh.

"Just passin' through," he said casually. "Sales trip."

"Oh," said the woman, taking her purse off of the bar and moving to the stool directly beside Dennis. "What do you sell?"

"Toner cartridges," Dennis said. "You know, for copy machines and such. Not very exciting, I'm afraid."

"Maybe not," said the woman. "But everyone needs 'em."

"That's absolutely right," Dennis said, glad that the woman hadn't denigrated his means of making a living and enthralled by the scent of her perfume. "Buy you a drink?"

"Why, that would be lovely." She touched the top of his hand with the tips of her fingers. "Thank you, Mr...?"

"Harvey," said Dennis. "Dennis Harvey. But, please call me Dennis."

"Thank you, Dennis. I'm Lily."

A white paper napkin suddenly spun onto the bar and slid to a halt in front of Lily. "Get you something?" said Nate, the bartender (Dennis made a habit of befriending every bartender he met; sometimes they were the only friends you had on the road).

"I'll have what he's having," Lily said, nodding her delectable chin at Dennis' drink.

"Gin and tonic," Dennis said.

"Sounds delicious," Lily responded. Nate gave her a polite nod and then gave Dennis a quick, approving glance that Dennis missed completely.

"So, how long you in town for?" Lily asked.

"Just today and tomorrow," said Dennis. "Heading back home Saturday morning."

"Home? Where's home?"

"Oxnard, California," Dennis said. "Not too far."

"Oxnard? What's an Oxnard?" Lily laughed.

"Oxnard is a beautiful little city by the sea," Dennis chuckled. "With a funny name." He laughed. "They've talked about changing it over the years. The name, I mean. Either to Channel Islands or Port Hueneme, like the naval base."

"What's a Why-Nee-Me?!" Lily asked with wide eyes. And they both laughed heartily as Nate brought Lily her drink.

The evening progressed and more drinks were had, more tales were spun and Dennis could feel a not unpleasant bond growing between him and his new friend. And then he felt something else: Her hand, crawling ever-so-slowly along his upper thigh.

"Dennis," Lily purred, slurring the "s" just a little bit. "Would you like to take me up to your room?"

Dennis put down his drink a little harder than he expected. The sound of the glass coming down on the wooden counter echoed throughout the mostly empty bar. Lily's hand came to a sudden halt. She giggled. She rested her cheek on his shoulder and stared up at him through smoldering dark eyes. Dennis sighed.

"There is nothing I'd like more, nothing I've ever wanted more," Dennis said. "But … I'm a happily married man."

"And I'm not married at all," Lily said. "And you're only going to be here one more day." Her hand began crabbing up his leg again. She took her head off his shoulder and put her lips right beside his ear. "Wouldn't you like to have some fun while you're here, Dennis?" she cooed.

He shivered with delight as her breath wisped into his ear. Still he resisted.

"I … I just can't, Lily," he said. "It's not that I don't want to…"

And then her hand was past his thigh and pressed against his zipper, and he felt himself harden almost instantly. And then her mouth was on his ear, on his cheek and on his mouth.

He quickly signed for the bill, grabbed her hand, and pulled her off the stool. She gave a surprised but happy "Ooop!" and together they headed for the elevator.

The last thing Dennis thought as the elevator doors closed them in and the heat of passion began to burn around them, was that he had never cheated on his wife before ... and he hoped it would be worth it.

CHAPTER SIX — June 4, 2015

You would have thought that somebody would have noticed him, if not at once, then at least shortly thereafter. But no one who came through the hotel bar in Tucson that night paid him the least bit of attention, despite the fact he was nearly six foot seven and weighed close to 325 pounds.

Simon Cadabra sat in the darkest corner of the Holiday Inn hotel bar, nursing a Kahlua and cream he'd purchased during happy hour nearly four hours earlier. The ice was all gone, of course, and the drink now resembled some kind of creamy, milk chocolate soup, but Cadabra didn't care. He didn't really like the taste of alcohol anyway and had only ordered the drink to better fit in. He did like the taste of appetizers, however, which was apparent from several empty plates smeared with buffalo sauce that were scattered on the table before him.

Cadabra had taken his seat in the dark corner when happy hour began at 5:00pm ("Half-Off all Well Drinks!"). He sipped on his Kahlua and quietly nibbled at the free "Nuclear Fire Wings" (kept warm in a silver tray beneath a browned yellow heat lamp) while he waited for the show to begin. Finally, toner cartridge salesman Dennis Harvey had predictably taken a seat at the bar and Lily Messerschmitt, who made a habit of picking up strange men at familiar bars, had predictably joined him. Cadabra had watched the liquor do its work and almost enjoyed it as the new friends became a carnal couple. When, at last, they had stood unsteadily from the bar and headed toward the elevator together, Cadabra allowed himself a grim smile. His goal was achieved; his work was done.

As the doors slid closed on the unfaithful Dennis Harvey and the surely STD-infected Lily Messerschmitt (yes, even Cadabra found it hard to believe that was her real name), Cadabra pushed his thick-lensed glasses higher onto his nose, waved the bartender over (his server had been sent home over an hour earlier due to the slow night) and asked to settle his tab.

The bill came to $7.50 and Cadabra left a five, three ones and two quarters on the plastic change tray and then pushed away from the table. Even though his chair scraped mightily as he stood, neither the bartender nor the bar's single other patron—another salesman (copy machines), not quite as lucky as Dennis in either business or love—seemed to notice Cadabra was mobile.

I'm surprised I even got a drink tonight, Cadabra thought as he passed through the front door of the bar and stepped into the hotel parking lot. *Nearly six foot seven, 325-pounds ... and apparently invisible.* It wasn't the first time in his life he'd been ignored. *If I would have been able to vanish like that on stage,* Cadabra thought, *instead of trying that goddamn immolation stunt, maybe I'd still be in Vegas.*

The moon wasn't quite full but it was bright and the evening was clear. It was warm and comfortable, even at this hour. It was the kind of night that made Cadabra wish he could spend more time in Arizona. He loved it where it was hot. Even in his plain, all-black suit, white shirt and shiny black shoes, Cadabra felt comfortable and safe.

Cadabra and the city bus arrived at the bus stop at almost exactly the same moment and Cadabra paid his fare and walked down the aisle toward the back as the bus pulled away from the curb. He sat in the very last row. A few moments after he took his seat, the cabin lights dimmed and the bus gathered speed.

Reaching into his coat pocket, Cadabra withdrew a shiny, new iPad mini. He opened the mail app, quickly tapped out a short e-mail, and hit send. Then the pad's screen went blank and the iPad went back to its cubby in his breast pocket. Cadabra watched the desert go by as the bus made occasional stops, taking on a few passengers, and belching out many more.

Twenty-five minutes later, there were only three other passengers on the bus, plus the bus driver, who turned and announced, "Next stop, last stop!" Cadabra sighed and imagined the other two passengers, whose destination was no doubt the same as his, giving similar exhausted sighs.

Finally, the bus turned off the main road and crept onto a parking lot covered by a corrugated aluminum roof and lit by bright but failing sodium vapor lights. A large metal sign with a green background and white letters announced: TUCSON MASS TRANSIT – OVERNIGHT LOT.

Once through the gate, the driver palmed the big steering wheel and the bus turned in a sweeping circle and then began to creep backwards—with a repetitive electronic beep stabbing the silence—as the driver shifted into reverse and backed into a three-sided garage, also made of corrugated aluminum.

"End of the Line," said the bus driver, killing the engine, grabbing his Alice Coopers'town baseball cap and grubby city-issued jacket, and stepping off the bus without looking back. Cadabra and the other two passengers remained where they were seated. Cadabra sighed with impatience. This was the part he hated most—the waiting.

A few seconds later, Cadabra caught sight of the driver through the windshield of the bus. He watched as the driver pulled the chain link gates closed (not without some effort) and locked them in place with a rusty chain and a comically enormous padlock. He gave the gates a shake and then faded into the darkness of the night. Cadabra watched him go, sighed again, tapped his fingers on his pant leg, and waited some more.

The sodium vapor lights in the parking lot suddenly flickered rapidly, tried valiantly to stay illuminated, and then went out. The darkness was complete. Cadabra felt the bus rock just a little—as though someone were shaking it by pushing on the sides—and then there was the grinding clank of metal and machinery. The next moment, Cadabra felt his stomach lurch as it always did when they began their descent.

The journey would take twelve minutes to reach its destination. Cadabra knew this not from a stopwatch but from counting in a whisper: "One thousand and one. One thousand and two. One thousand and three" and so on. Each time he had counted, he would get to just under 720, or just over 720 depending on how fast he counted, before they arrived at The Office. He also knew, or had been told, that The Office was exactly 6.66 miles beneath the surface, which meant they were traveling at just over thirty miles an hour. He had no idea why he knew these things but they, and too many other factoids like them, were stuck in his mind forever.

Almost exactly twelve minutes later, and with another cacophony of clanking machinery and grinding gears, the platform supporting the bus came to a jerking halt and a roll up garage door opened before them. Cadabra had to shield his eyes from the sudden bright white light that flooded the elevator like a supernova. He and the other two passengers stood, walked zombie-like to the folding door, and stepped down, out of the bus.

As he stepped down, Cadabra realized that he recognized one of the other two passengers.

"Evening, Johnson," he said.

"Evening, Cadabra."

They entered the retina-burning glow of stark white artificial light.

There were thousands of them, tens of thousands, hundreds of thousands, millions maybe. And they were all exactly the same: gray, sterile and dull. Office cubicles, as far as the eye could see, rolling back and to both sides until they blurred together like pixels on a TV screen.

Telephones rang constantly and from every direction, their shrill electronic bells buzzing through the air like a chainsaw. Cadabra felt his soul go dry at the sight and he knew that was exactly the effect they were going for. He began walking toward the cubicle he inhabited, and grimly acknowledged once again that it was going to be quite a long walk. While his cubicle wasn't nearly as far away as others, it was still quite a haul and there was nothing but other cubicles to hold his interest as he went.

He walked through the warm, still air of The Office, glancing into the passing cubicles and seeing nothing he hadn't seen before. They were just gray walls. No photos, no knick-knacks personalizing the area, no way to identify one cubicle from another. Just gray walls and cheap black office furniture. Within those walls, everyone was busy at work, either clacking away on their computer keyboards or talking emotionlessly on the phone. No one was having a friendly chat and no one was standing around the water cooler (mainly because there wasn't one). Occasionally, Cadabra saw someone with a bottle of water and he wondered what they had done to earn such a reward. Even those people looked bored and miserable and Cadabra was unsurprised to find that he himself felt both.

At last, he came to a yet another unremarkable gray cubicle with a brown nametag with white letters cut into it (in the plainest font possible): S CADABRA. He sat down in the bargain-basement rolling office chair there and sighed with relief despite its uncomfortableness. It had been a long day that was only destined to repeat itself tomorrow.

There was no bottle of water on his desk.

"Cadabra! My office!" an abrasive voice screeched. Cadabra winced as though someone had taken a cheese-grater to his elbow. He looked up to see his Supervisor, Clay Watkins, rushing past, his finger hooked behind him, harshly beckoning. Cadabra sighed. He relished being called to Watkins' office about as much as he relished drinking napalm.

Or burning myself alive on stage in front of three thousand people, he thought.

"Right there, boss," he said. He felt his shoulders droop and his spine bowed like a marshmallow harp bow.

He took a deep breath, let it out slowly, and headed toward Watkins' office.

Which was right next to the rolling garage door where the bus had dropped him off just a few minutes earlier.

Of course.

CHAPTER SEVEN

Clay Watkins was an officious little prick: a skinny, gnarled stick of a man with a sprout of dirty gray hair that sat atop his head like a dying jelly fish left to dry in the sun. Cadabra (and all of his fellow cubicle workers as well) avoided Watkins when at all possible at The Office, but it wasn't often possible. Watkins had a preternatural sense of making himself present when it was the least possibly convenient. Cadabra understood that was what part of The Office was all about—this wasn't meant to be a happy place—but it didn't make it the slightest bit easier to deal with the man.

Watkins' office wasn't much more than another cubicle with higher walls. It was the same drab color, the same cheap office furniture, the same thin gray carpet. There were no personal items anywhere to be found: no photos, no "World's Best Dad" coffee mugs, no cheesy "Employee of the Month" award plaques. Cadabra entered the mind-numbing dullness to find Watkins pulling a manila folder out of a gray metal filing cabinet with impossibly deep drawers. Seeing the man struggling with the massive drawer brought Cadabra's dislike of his supervisor to the forefront. He was one of those skinny, bony, hawk-faced men who made up for his lack of body weight with an overly aggressive personality.

"It's time for your performance review," Watkins said, tossing the plain manila folder onto his cluttered desk.

"I just *had* a performance review!" Cadabra protested.

"Time for another," said Watkins indifferently. He sat down at his desk, perched a pair of cheater glasses on his nose, and opened the folder. He snatched a pencil from the plain black cup on his desk, licked the tip lasciviously, and touched the lead to one of the papers inside.

"Says here you just got back from assignment," Watkins said. "Says it was successful."

"Yeah," Cadabra said. "I sent you an e-mail about it the moment it was complete."

Watkins ignored him, sitting back in his chair, which squeaked alarmingly despite Watkins' thin frame, and interlocked his fingers across his chest. "Tell me about it."

Cadabra sighed. "Standard cheating husband scenario," he said. "I arranged a meeting at a bar and they did the rest."

Watkins lowered his chin and stared at Cadabra over his cheaters. "Any hitches?"

"Not a one. Textbook example."

Watkins made a couple of checkmarks on the paperwork before him, nodded thoughtfully, and gave his pencil another lick. Cadabra knew the checkmarks meant nothing. They were all for show.

The chair squeaked in agony again as Watkins leaned forward and slapped the folder closed. He tossed the pencil carelessly on his desk and whisked off his cheaters in what he probably thought was a very dramatic movement. *It isn't*, Cadabra thought.

"You don't seem very pleased." Watkins said. "Classic success story like this one. Show some pride, man."

"It was easy," Cadabra said. "Too easy."

"Really?" Watkins asked with a reptilian smirk.

"Really," confirmed Cadabra. "And it's really not fair. You tempt a guy who's been married for over twenty years with a woman who's like a horny porn star and that's gonna happen. That guy had only seen women that beautiful in magazines. Suddenly, there's one at his elbow and she's whispering sweet nothings in his ear? That and the six gin and tonics they drank—apiece, not between them—yeah, that'll get a guy in trouble."

"So, you think we should have sent him somebody … uglier?" Watkins asked in disbelief.

"Not ugly," Cadabra said. "But more realistic. Somebody more in his league. That guy is going to go home and give his wife the clap and why? Because we tempted him with pure gold when it would have been fairer to try silver."

Watkins shook his head. "You're a piece of work, Cadabra. What makes you think The Office plays fair?"

"I understand that isn't our nature, sir," Cadabra said. "It just doesn't seem right."

"You're never going to move on until you get with the program," Watkins said. "You know that, don't you?"

"I know."

"Are you afraid to move on?" Watkins asked. "Is that the problem here? Are you not doing the work because you're afraid? Do you need to talk to somebody in HR?"

"No, sir," Cadabra bristled. "I *am* doing the work, but sometimes I just have questions about the way it's being done."

"Well, lucky for you, it's not up to you. Your job is to just to do what we tell you. You got that?"

"Yes, sir," Cadabra said. But he was thinking *Screw you, asshole.*

Watkins snorted noisily, sucking all kinds of nastiness into his throat and then swallowing it effortlessly. He sat back in his chair again, eyeing Cadabra, occasionally narrowing his eyes. Cadabra took it as long as he could stand and then asked, "Was there something else, sir?"

Watkins sat forward suddenly, opened a lower drawer in his desk and withdrew a blood-red manila folder. The words TOP SECRET were stamped across it in military-style lettering. Cadabra found himself shocked and fascinated by the folder's bright color and its bold font. It was by far the most ornate thing he'd ever seen in The Office.

"This is your new assignment," Watkins said. "Read it, learn it, memorize it, achieve it."

Cadabra's fingers crabbed across the desk and pulled the red folder toward him. He opened it and scanned the first page. As he read, he felt his emotions change from interest to puzzlement and, finally, to disgust.

"What is this?" he asked quietly.

"I just told you," Watkins said, his tone dripping supervisorial venom. "It's your new assignment. Straight from the top."

"Why me?"

"You've been here long enough," Watkins said. "This is your ticket out of here."

Cadabra swallowed and his suddenly dry throat clicked alarmingly. He needed a bottle of water more now than ever.

"But ..." he managed, his mind roiling over the contents of the red folder. "But ... they want ..."

"That's right," Watkins grinned like an insane villain in a Frank Miller comic book. "They want you to kill a little girl."

CHAPTER EIGHT — June 5, 2015

"Has anyone seen Anjelica?" asked Mother Superior Mary Shelley as she entered the sparse dining room at the Our Mother of Mighty Redemption Convent in Las Vegas, Nevada. The four nuns seated at the table looked up in unison, frowned and shook their heads, then went back to their paper plates and steaming Hot Pockets, fresh out of the microwave oven.

"If you see her, please let her know I'm looking for her," Mary Shelley said. The lunching nuns nodded again and then continued to wait for their Hot Pockets to cool so they could be eaten without the threat of third degree burns on their mouths or tongues.

Where has that girl gone to? Mary Shelley thought. Even though she knew Anjelica was safe here in the convent, she couldn't help but feel a tiny pang of panic. The girl had been with them for four years now, ever since she mysteriously appeared on the doorstep, and Mary Shelley had come to love her like a daughter. As confident as she was of the girl's safety, she never forgot the fact that this *was* downtown Las Vegas and not the most wholesome place in the world to call home.

That's why we must always be ready, Mary Shelley thought. *Because* that *day will come.*

Mary Shelley walked down the main hallway of the convent and peeked into each room. There was the laundry room, No Anjelica there. The kitchen; no Anjelica there either. The office, the bathroom, the study, their quarters. Still no Anjelica. Mary Shelley sighed deeply and tried to stay calm. There was one place she hadn't looked and she'd found Anjelica there in the past.

The chapel.

She hurried down the hallway, stepped into the foyer and over to the richly decorated and darkly stained double doors that led into the convent's relatively small chapel. She heaved the doors open (they seemed to be getting heavier every year) and entered.

It was a small but functional chapel, used mostly for individual prayer but also for the occasional event whenever the roving bishop or monsignor might drop by. Four sets of pews were lined up on each side of a narrow walkway that lead to a low stage. There, a life-size mahogany statue of Jesus on the cross rose up from the floor and reached in agony toward the sky. Or as high was he could reach with his hands nailed onto the crossbeam. A crown of thorns was pushed down tightly on his head, rivulets of wooden blood, sanded smooth and varnished to a bright shine, dripped down his tortured face. His face was a mask of misery, his eyes like those of a man doomed to die painfully rather than a savior cleansing the souls of all of humanity. Mary Shelley found herself once again wondering why crucifixes such as this one focused so much on the pain rather than the hope that the Lord had given them. *But we need to know how difficult his sacrifice was*, she thought, *in order to appreciate what he did for us all.*

The heavy wooden doors swung slowly closed behind her and, for a moment, the chapel was bathed in total darkness. Before long, Mary Shelley's eyes began to adjust and she saw ("Thank God!") a dim, white figure sitting in the front pew.

Anjelica.

Mary Shelley smiled with relief as she walked quietly to the first pew and sat beside the little girl. She stared down at her accidental ward and felt a wave of love wash over her. Anjelica's blonde hair, golden now but showing the first hints of darkness that would make it dirty blonde in a year or two, fell to her shoulders and curled back up in bouncy little hooks. Freshly cut just yesterday by Sister Tomasa, it shimmered in the dim light that came through the stained-glass windows that surrounded them. She wore a cute but simple dress—patterned with images of playful kittens—and a pair of Spongebob Squarepants flip-flops.

Anjelica sat silently, not really acknowledging Mary Shelley's presence but not ignoring it, either. She stared with eyes bright with curiosity at the face of Jesus on the cross, a mix of utter sadness and grim gratitude apparent on her face.

Mary Shelley just sat and watched her for a moment. She was so precious, and so wonderful, and Mary Shelley thought again about the promise she'd made to protect her, to do whatever she had to do to make sure the girl was safe. Always.

And we're ready to do just that, she thought, *when the time comes.*

"What ya doin', honey?" Mary Shelley asked the little girl, putting her arm around her shoulders.

"Just thinkin'," Anjelica said.

"About what?"

"I try to think what he was thinking," Anjelica said. "Hanging there."

Mary Shelley looked up at the crucifix herself. "I don't know, honey," she said. "But I know that he did it for us."

"That's what I mean," Anjelica said. "He did it for us. So, what was he thinking? He was dying for our sins but do you think he wondered if it was worth it? If *we* were worth it?"

Unbidden tears welled up in Mary Shelley's eyes. Such deep thoughts from such a young girl. Not even eight years old, and she was already asking the big questions. "I think he thought that we were," she said after a moment. "Worth it, I mean."

"I want to be," Anjelica said quietly. "I want to be worth it."

Another wave of love warmed Mary Shelley's smile. "You will be, honey," she said. "I just know you will be."

They sat there for a few seconds, in the presence of their God, their thoughts silent, questioning, and mysterious. After a moment, Mary Shelley asked, "Hey, how about a peanut butter sandwich?"

"Strawberry jelly?" Anjelica said, finally taking her eyes off the crucifix.

Mary Shelley frowned. "I think we're out," she said, feeling more disappointed than Anjelica appeared to be. "We've got grape. And honey, I think, unless Sister Cecelia ate it all again."

"Honey!" Anjelica said brightly. And leapt off the pew and ran toward the doors.

Mother Superior Mary Shelley sat alone for a moment, feeling the weight of responsibility bearing down on her. It was a responsibility that she was honored to call her own

After a moment, she stood, crossed herself, and followed Anjelica out the door.

CHAPTER NINE

Sandra Bullock pushed herself up off the muddy ground, climbed weakly out of what looked like a primordial swamp and limped painfully away. The end credits started to roll.

And Richard Keane, Private Investigator, realized that there were tears of joy and triumph streaming down his cheeks.

He wiped away the tears with the back of his hand, picked up the Sony remote control from his desk and punched the OFF button. The 60" television screen across the room winked off. Keane tossed the remote back on the desk, took his feet out of the desk drawer he'd been using as a footrest, and slid it closed. He sat for a moment and contemplated the movie he'd just watched. *Damn*, he thought. *That was a good one.*

He rested his arms on the desktop and thoughtfully stroked his chin. *Now what?*

He could read a book. There was an endless supply of books to read on the Kindle next to the telephone. Keane had never been a voracious reader, but he enjoyed the classics: Chandler, Hammett, Spillane. And he'd become a fan of the new modern masters: Parker, Child, Grafton. Or he could read a newspaper. Virtually any newspaper in the world was loaded on that Kindle. Or magazine. Keane was certain he could find something interesting to read if he felt like it.

If he felt like it.

He didn't feel like it.

He could watch another movie. Or television show. Or news program. Again, virtually anything he might want to see could be found on that 60" TV.

If he felt like it.

But he didn't.

He decided to see what was on the menu for lunch, kick back at his desk and listen to some music on the PC while he ate.

He crawled out of his desk chair and padded in white-socked feet over to the short refrigerator against the wall.

Like the 60" TV, the Kindle, and the PC, this was another new addition to his original office back on Sunset Boulevard. He didn't have a refrigerator then, couldn't possibly afford to have one. But he had one here. He reached down, opened the door and peered inside, pleased to find that the two beers he drank last night had been mysteriously replaced with two fresh ones and there was a wrapped sandwich sitting on the top shelf. "Ham and Cheese (Swiss)" was scrawled across the brown paper wrapper in ornate but quite legible handwriting. He snatched the sandwich and a bottle of Coca-Cola (also thoughtfully replenished) and took both of them over to "The View."

Setting the bottle of Coke on the metal filing cabinet near where the front door used to be way back in 1954, Keane peeled open the sandwich wrapping—exposing what looked like an absolutely delicious sandwich—and took a bite. He chewed thoughtfully and appreciatively, staring out at the huge expanse of twinkling stars that made up what he called "The View." It was still breathtaking, even after all this time. *Another nice upgrade*, he thought, taking another bite. He enjoyed the sandwich's amazing savory flavor for a moment and then turned around to survey his office. *I gotta admit, I like the upgrades*, he thought, taking in his surroundings.

The office was exactly the same size, shape, and color that it had been back in 1954. The coat rack still stood like a sentry in the far-left corner and Keane's tan trench coat still hung there. His fedora was perched on its topmost branch, a circular black hole a little bigger than a dime gaping on the left side of the crown where Mukasa's thug had put a bullet through it. The desk was there, with its high-backed leather chair (Keane's office chair) and the two guest chairs in front.

What was sitting on the desktop had changed considerably. Whereas before there was only the heavy iron typewriter, a phone and a desk fan, there was now a sleek personal computer, a digital multi-lined phone (which still never rang) and a Dyson Airblade fan. The Kindle, resting by the telephone, was also new.

Then, on the right wall, there was the television with all its channels; a 60" inch digital monster with incredible definition that made it seem to be more of a window looking into another world than a video screen. Keane had spent more hours watching that TV than he cared to admit but, boy, was he glad to have it.

He turned back to "The View" and once again was enveloped in its wonder. Because, where the fourth wall of his office used to be, the wall that separated Keane's office from the hallway, was … nothing. It was as if that wall had been simply cut away with the swipe of the galaxy's biggest scalpel. In its place was what seemed to Keane to be some kind of transparent window or energy source, like he'd seen on *Star Trek* or some other science fiction show. He couldn't see it; it didn't reflect any images off its surface. It was just *there*. Touching it was like touching glass. And beyond it was nothing but stars. Up, down, left, right, as far as the eye could see. Nothing but stars glittering on the black background of space.

Keane often had the feeling that his office was floating in the middle of the universe, hundreds of light years from anyone or anything else, and that he was resoundingly *alone*.

And he wasn't too far wrong.

Keane finished his sandwich and quickly drank down the cola he'd almost forgotten about. For what he thought had to be the ten millionth time, he wondered *What the hell am I doing here?* and (for what was probably also the ten millionth time) he received no answer. He tossed the sandwich wrapper in a wastebasket by his desk, dropped the Coke bottle through a round hole cut into a square box that read RECYCABLES, and sat back down at his desk.

Maybe a little Katy Perry, he thought, grabbing the mouse and clicking around on his screen. After a few moments, the majestic sounds of "Roar" filled the room through unseen speakers and Keane rocked back in his leather chair and enjoyed the empowering pop anthem.

Keane had just started dropping off to sleep when a soft, wet *POP* brought him back to full wakefulness and he found himself staring across the room at a small plump infant, unbound by gravity, floating a full three or four feet off the ground. The infant stared back at him, its face impossibly adult with knowing eyes and a mouth Keane almost expected to see a cigar screwed into. The pinkish skin on its tiny infant body was baby smooth but Keane thought that a face like that ought to have a five o'clock shadow and maybe even some acne scarring. The infant was enrobed in a flowing white sheet or blanket that really had no reason to stay where it was but hung on the baby as though Velcro'd there. The small, bird-like wings protruding from its back flapped rapidly, almost like a hummingbird's, as it hovered there patiently, mid-air.

Keane killed the Katy Perry song, sighed deeply, and sat forward. "Well, if it isn't Buster the Cherub," he said. "To what do I owe the pleasure?"

CHAPTER TEN

Buster's face wasn't the only thing disturbingly adult about him. His voice, too, was deep and rich, the voice of a radio announcer or film trailer narrator. It was a voice that fit the face, but not the infantile body. After all this time, Keane still wasn't used to it.

"How ya doin', chief?" Buster asked, buzzing over and settling himself in one of the two guest chairs. Keane had to scoot forward, sit on the edge of his chair, and peer over the opposite side of the desk to see him.

"Oh, I'm just hunky dory," Keane said. "Loving life. Or whatever this is. What's new with you?"

"Just checking in," Buster said. "Been awhile."

"About two weeks by my calculations."

"You know time means nothing up here," Buster said. "How's the chow?"

"Ham and cheese today," Keane told him. "I liked it."

"Good. I like to hear that."

They sat quietly for a moment, the only sound in the room the nearly silent hissing of the Airblade at work. Then, Buster said: "Look, you've been here awhile. We've got some things to discuss."

"Discuss away," Keane said. "You're the social worker."

"Don't call me that!" Buster snapped. "You know I hate that."

Keane only smiled.

"So, listen. You know why you're here, right?" Buster continued.

"Do we really have to go through this again?"

"Yeah, we do." Buster said. "There's a reason."

Keane sighed. "If you insist," he said. "But let me get a beer first. I'm gonna need a little alcohol if we're gonna do this again." He stood and walked around the cherub to the fridge, grabbed a Sierra Nevada Pale Ale off the top shelf. Another perk of the new arrangement: better beer. "You want one?"

"You know I can't have one," Buster said bitterly.

"I do," Keane said, chuckling. "I do indeed know that."

"So," Buster said, as Keane settled in his chair. "You know why you're here, right?"

"I know why you *tell* me I'm here," Keane said.

Buster shook his head in exasperation.

"Because …" Keane continued in a near sing-song tone. "Before that son of a bitch Mukasa had me shot in the head, I wasn't a very good man. I wasn't a bad man, but I wasn't a very good man. So, when I died, you folks had a hard time deciding whether to send me to Heaven or to Hell."

"The Light or The Dark," Buster corrected. "We don't say 'Heaven' or 'Hell.'"

"Whatever," Keane went on. "So now I'm here in Purgatory …"

"Not Purgatory," Buster corrected. "We don't use that term, either, as you well know. You're Betwixt."

Keane laughed out loud. "Oh, yes. 'Betwixt.' Because that's so much better than Purgatory."

"I've told you many times, it's not about an individual religion," Buster said. "It's about what *is*, what's real. So no religious terms. No Heaven, no Hell, no Purgatory. No God. No Devil."

Keane chuckled again and shook his head. "All right, whatever you say. So, I'm stuck here, trapped Betwixt, because I stole candy as a kid and because I cheated on my taxes."

"And your fiancée," Buster said.

Keane glared at him. "Yes," he said. "That."

"And some other things," Buster continued. "And, yes, that's why you're here." He fidgeted in the chair, wiped his chin (*right where the five o'clock shadow should be*, Keane thought) and then looked directly into Keane's eyes.

"But do you know how to get out of here?" Buster asked finally.

"Jesus Christ!" Keane spat, livid. "I've been asking you that for fifty years!"

"No swearing," Buster said. "And time has no …"

"Yes, yes, I know. Time has no meaning here. So, no, Buster, I do not know how to get out of here but I sure as sh …"

The cherub waggled his stubby finger.

"…I sure as heck would like to find out."

"Good," said Buster, nodding his head with what Keane realized was great satisfaction. "Good. Because we've got an assignment for you."

"An assignment?"

"Yes," said the plump, pinkish little cherub. "We want you to save a little girl."

CHAPTER ELEVEN

The bottle of beer stopped halfway to Keane's mouth. He stared at his visitor quizzically. "A little girl?" he asked.

Buster nodded. "It should be an easy assignment," he said. "I've seen much worse handed down, trust me." He fluttered his wings, lifted up from the seat a bit, and then floated back down, apparently getting more comfortable. "Your assignment is simply to move her from her current location to the mission in Santa Barbara as quickly and as safely as possible."

"Sounds simple enough," Keane said. "Where's she at now?"

"Las Vegas."

"Vegas? This just keeps getting better. What time is her flight?"

"No flight," Buster said. "You're driving,"

"So," Keane mused. "In order to escape from Betwixt, I have to be a chauffeur?"

Buster shrugged, his plump little shoulders rising. "A little," he said. "But you're more of a guardian. Your assignment is to make sure she makes the journey safely."

"Vegas to Santa Barbara, huh? That's only like a five-hour drive."

"Closer to six," Buster said. "Depending on traffic."

"Traffic?" Keane asked, thinking of the horrific lines of unmoving cars he'd seen on the television and how insanely worse it was today than in 1954. "Are you sure we can't fly? Better yet, can't you just blink her there or something? Save us both some time and trouble."

"No," Buster said. "It doesn't work that way."

"Of course," Keane scoffed. "The Lord works in mysterious ways."

"Don't say Lord."

"*Someone* works in mysterious ways," Keane corrected. "So, let me get this straight: You want me to take this girl … how old is she, by the way?"

"She's almost eight."

"Perfect," Keane rolled his eyes. "So you want me to take this girl from Las Vegas to Santa Barbara, in a car, and my only job is to get her there in one piece?"

"That's the gist of it," Buster agreed.

"Piece of cake!" Keane said. "Let's get this show on the road!" He set his beer back on the desktop and stood, reaching for his coat.

"Not so fast," Buster said. "There are some rules we should discuss."

"Here we go," Keane said, dropping back into his chair. "Lay it on me. Wait! Let me guess: I have to do this in a Ford Pinto!"

"No," Buster said. "Actually, we want you to choose the car. It would make sense for you to drive your old Cambridge since you're used to it, but …"

"Sixty-nine Dodge Charger," Keane interrupted quickly. "Preferably black."

"You've never driven a car built after 1951!" Buster protested.

"Don't care," Keane said. "I love that car. I want to drive that car. All the badasses drive that car. Wesley Snipes drives one in *Blade*, Michael Westen drives one in *Burn No-tice*. Mr. Chapel drives one in *Vengeance Unlimited*. I want a black 1969 Dodge Charger. Or no deal."

"Seriously?" Buster asked.

"Not a hundred percent," Keane admitted. "But do what you can do. Okay?"

"Worst mistake we ever made," Buster groused. "Giving you that television."

"How else was I going to keep up with the world?" Keane said. "And, anyway, it's not just the TV. Badasses in books drive them, too. H.B. Fist, for example. And his is re-fitted for space travel!" A dreamy look came over his face. "Hey, what if …"

"Fine!" Buster said quickly. "You can have a 1969 Dodge Charger. And, no, it's *not* being re-fitted for space travel."

"Black?"

"Fine," Buster said again.

Keane was thrilled. "All right, then. So, you want me to drive a little girl from Las Vegas to Santa Barbara *in a*

1969 Dodge Charger. That's more of a vacation than an assignment. So, what's the catch?"

"You gotta make four stops between Las Vegas and Santa Barbara: Baker, Lake Dolores, Calico Ghost Town and Vasquez Rocks."

Keane shook his head in confusion. "Why?"

Buster just shrugged again.

"Mysterious ways," Keane said, rolling his eyes again. "Figures. And what are we supposed to do at each of these stops?"

"The girl will know."

"Swell. Anything else?"

"Oh, just that the forces of evil will be trying to stop you," Buster said casually. "By any means possible."

"You're shittin' me."

"I'm not," Buster said. "And watch your mouth." He ran a tiny hand across his smooth cheek. "We don't know what to expect, but we're certain that there will be a concentrated effort to prevent you from reaching Santa Barbara. But we're not sending you in empty handed."

There was another soft pop like the one that had awakened Keane a few minutes before and suddenly there was a .45 caliber handgun on the desktop. Keane recognized it instantly. It was a 1911 .45 ACP, the same weapon Keane's father had been issued during World War I and the very weapon Keane himself had carried in World War II. It was, in fact, the same weapon that Keane had carried in the holster beneath his left arm until his untimely death.

His father had nicknamed it "Whisper" for reasons that he had never explained to his son.

"Wondered where that went," Keane said, picking up the .45 and examining it closely.

"You didn't have much use for it here," said Buster.

"I would think not," Keane said, admiring the gun from every angle. It looked exactly the same as it had in 1954. "I missed you, sweetheart."

"It's your gun," Buster said, "But with one major modification: It will never run out of ammo. As long as you can pull the trigger, the gun will continue to fire."

"That's a good modification," Keane said. "But can bullets stop the forces of evil?"

"Yes," Buster said with a smile. "They can." He reached into the folds of his white cloth swaddle and removed something inside.

"Got something in your diaper?" Keane asked.

"Very funny," Buster said. "And then there's this." He tossed a short cylinder onto the desktop and it rolled over to the edge and fell where Keane caught it and examined it.

It was a bullet that appeared as though it were made of glass. Inside was a roiling, fiery substance that looked like boiling hot lava. Keane expected it to be hot to the touch as well but instead it was cool and vibrated gently with harnessed power.

"What's this?" he asked.

"That is the Hell Shell," Buster said.

"Did you just say Hell?" Keane asked, eyes wide.

"That's what it's called," Buster said. "The Hell Shell. It is good only once but, whomever you shoot with that bullet will be sent directly to The Darkness."

"To Hell," Keane said, winking.

"To the Darkness," Buster insisted. "It's called the Hell Shell because its interior looks like what you'd expect Hell to look like, if such a place actually existed."

Keane chuckled. "Okay, what else?'

"I think that's it," Buster said.

"And what happens if we don't make it?"

Buster shrugged again.

"Mysterious ways," Keane groused.

"No," Buster said. "I really don't know. Maybe the world will come to an end, maybe it won't. Maybe nothing. I just don't know."

"So why me?"

"Whattaya mean, why you?"

"I mean, why me?" Keane asked. "I'm a gumshoe, not a babysitter. Why choose me? There's got to be a hundred other people better qualified for this type of work than I am. A thousand."

The Cherub only shrugged.

"Mysterious ways," Keane said again, shaking his head. "And what about you? You comin' with?"

"Can't," Buster said. "Not allowed to help. I can offer advice but I will not be available to help you in any way."

"Well, that sucks," Keane said.

"Yeah," Buster said. "It does. But you'll be fine."

Keane stood, walked over to the coat rack and slipped into his trench coat. He slid his feet into the shoes at the coat rack's base and finally popped his fedora atop his full head of black hair. A few loose strands poked out of the hole in its side.

"So, what are we standing here flapping our gums for?" Keane said. "Let's get on with it!"

And, with another of those weird, soft pops, Keane's office was suddenly empty.

Reverend Mother Mary Shelley stacked another can of Del Monte peaches on top of the growing pyramid of canned goods that had been donated to the convent for the homeless. One of the nice things about being in Las Vegas was that there was always leftover food at the casinos and they were more than willing to donate the extra to the cause.

Mary Shelley stood back and admired her handiwork. There must have been three or four hundred cans in that stack, and yet it was as sturdy and as solid as if they had been glued together. That was by design. It was imperative that none of the cans fell and got dented. She'd seen swollen, botulism-contaminated cans before and knew of the sickness, or worse, they might bring. The last thing she wanted was for her convent to be responsible for the death of one of those less fortunate.

She topped the growing stack with one more can of pears and gave the tin pyramid a satisfied look of approval. There was enough food in the storage room to last a year, easily. *If the rapture suddenly happens,* Mary Shelley thought, *there will be plenty for those left behind.*

The door opened behind her and Sister Cecilia poked her head in. "Reverend Mother?" she said, "There's someone here to see you."

"Oh? Who?"

"Someone from the City," Sister Cecilia said. "Didn't say what it was regarding."

Probably someone looking for one of the homeless, Mary Shelley thought. People from the government, often the police, occasionally stopped with questions about suspected shoplifters or with family members searching for loved ones. It was Mary Shelley's personal policy to help when she could. Not only did she feel it was beneficial for everyone to weed out the bad eggs, it felt wonderful to reunite someone with their family.

She took one last glance at the tin can pyramid, brushed her hands together to knock off the dust, and followed Sister Cecelia to the front door. There, a very large man in a black suit stood waiting, a briefcase in one hand and a patient smile plastered on his face. He looked vaguely familiar but Mary Shelley couldn't place him.

Alarm bells went off in Mary Shelley's head. This was not the usual government visit.

"I am Mother Superior Mary Shelley," she said, holding out her hand. "How may I help you?"

The man did not take the offered hand and his patient smile vanished. Mary Shelley's alarm level increased. "Sister Shelley, my name is Simon Cadabra. I'm with Child Protective Services. I'm here looking for a young girl," the man said.

Mary Shelley tried not to let her alarm show through. "It's *Reverend Mother* Mary Shelley," she said. "Who is this girl you're looking for?"

"Her name is Anjelica Martinez," Cadabra said. "She's about eight years old. Her parents have been on the lam for about four years now. I can't go into details, but let's just say the law recently caught up with them. They tell us that they dropped their daughter off here shortly before they skipped town and that's the last anybody has seen of her. I was wondering if you might have any ideas as to her whereabouts."

"Pardon me," Mary Shelley said. "What did you say your name was?"

The man smiled politely. "Simon Cadabra," he said. "With Child Protective Services."

"I'm sorry, Mr. Cadabra," Mary Shelley said. "But there aren't any children here. And I don't recognize the name. Martinez, did you say?"

A man in a stained rock'n'roll t-shirt and tattered blue jeans walked up behind Cadabra and stopped at his right side. Cadabra paid him no attention. Mary Shelley couldn't see the newcomer's face but assumed he was one of her homeless drop-ins, stopping by for free soup and bread. A split second later the man's body odor hit her nostrils and she was certain he had lived on the streets for a very long time.

"Yes, Martinez," Cadabra replied, offering yet another friendly smile. "Anjelica Martinez."

"No, doesn't ring a bell," Mary Shelley said, and was surprised to see yet another man, this one in a dusty and well-worn black suit, step up on Cadabra's left. The smell of unwashed bodies seemed to intensify but still Cadabra paid them no heed. *What are they doing here so early?* Mary Shelley thought. *Evening meal isn't served for another hour.*

The alarm bells grew louder. Something was wrong here.

"You're sure?" Cadabra asked. "There's no Anjelica Martinez here?"

"I'm certain," Mary Shelley said. "If there had been a child dropped off here, we would have notified the local authorities and they would have taken it from there. I'm afraid Mr. and Mrs. Martinez are fabricating a story."

Cadabra pursed his lips and Mary Shelley sensed that he wasn't buying anything she said, and suddenly there was yet another homeless man standing just behind him, intensifying the moldy odor. Mary Shelley felt her hackles rise. These three men were either spaced out on drugs or mentally incapacitated. They stood silently behind Cadabra, their faces down, simply standing and listening and waiting.

And, with a burst of adrenaline, she realized that they were with him.

"I'm sorry you feel that way," Cadabra said. "Do you mind if I come in, have a look around?"

"Do you have a warrant?" Mary Shelley said, and realized she'd probably asked that too quickly.

"Do I need a warrant?" Cadabra asked. "Is there something you're hiding, Reverend Mother?"

One of the homeless men looked up briefly, but long enough for Mary Shelley to catch his eyes. There were no pupils visible, the eyes were entirely white, like a boiled egg, and Mary Shelley suddenly realized that what she had been smelling wasn't unwashed bodies and filthy clothes.

It was rot.

Because these men weren't on drugs or mentally ill. In fact, in all probability, they were dead.

And, with another warm burst of adrenaline, she realized that *this* was the moment they had warned her would come. *This* was the moment they had prepared for throughout the four years since Anjelica had been delivered to them. This was the moment she feared more than anything else in her entire life.

It was here. It was now.

And they were ready.

She took a breath as if to answer Cadabra's last question and then slammed the door in his face, setting the three deadbolts as quickly as she could. She could hear Cadabra roar with anger and the door shuddered violently as he threw his massive bulk against it. Mary Shelley gave a little cry of fear as the door cracked somewhere with a splintering sound but held … for now.

"Code Red!" Mary Shelley screamed. *"Code Red!"* She pried a large crucifix off the wall next to the door, revealing a round, illuminated red button. She slapped it hard with the heel of her hand. Alarm klaxons began blaring and red emergency lights flashed throughout the building and she could hear the others in the convent snapping to attention.

It was here. And it was now.

Cadabra hit the door again. He bellowed curses and threats but the door held solid.

Mary Shelley raced down the hallway and almost crashed into Sister Cecelia as she was bursting out of the laundry room.

"Is it happening?" Cecilia asked.

"It's happening," Mary Shelley told her.

"We're ready," Cecelia said. Her arm came out of the folds of her habit and revealed a shining MAC-11 sub-compact machine pistol gripped tightly in her hands. The weapon gleamed with well-kept maintenance and sheer determined malignance.

"We better be," Mary Shelley said, pushing past her. "Take your post."

Cecelia ran back down the hallway toward the front door. Mary Shelley stepped into the laundry and found Sisters Caterina and Hildegard already inside. As she had been trained, Caterina had pulled the big Kenmore washing machine out of its spot, revealing a hidden cabinet behind it. The cabinet door was wide open, and Caterina was passing another MAC-11 to Hildegard who took it, checked it, and turned to exit. She nodded to Mary Shelley and put a hand on her shoulder. "We're ready," she said. "We'll protect her."

"I know," Mary Shelley said. "We must."

As Hildegard left the laundry room, Caterina passed Mary Shelley a weapon of her own. Mary Shelley took it, checked it, and said, "Close that up and get to your post. I'll be with Anjelica."

"Understood," Caterina said, taking the last MAC-11 out of the safe and closing the heavy door with a metal clang.

Mary Shelley stepped into the hall again, glancing briefly at the front door and listening intently. The klaxons had stopped blaring and it was generally quiet. There was no more pounding at the front door but Mary Shelley didn't for a moment think that meant this was over. Even if the man at the door—Mr. Cadabra—had given up and gone away (which was unlikely), he, or somebody like him, would be back soon enough.

Mary Shelley's only real surprise was that it taken them this long to come for Anjelica.

There was a sudden shattering of glass and a brief burst of machine-gun fire from the dining room, followed by a blast that shook the walls. Mary Shelley's heart sank. She envisioned the beautiful, floor-to-ceiling stained-glass window in the dining room now shattered into a million tiny bits and she wondered how Sister Johanna had fared. The dining room was her post. Had she held them back or had she been overrun? There was no time to consider the outcome. Mary Shelley ran toward the chapel, pried open the massive double doors there, and closed them behind her.

It was the safest room in the building. There were three large stained-glass windows on each of the outside walls, but they were fifteen feet above ground and made access to the interior difficult. The thick double doors were the only way in or out and Mary Shelley locked them, and then slipped a large wooden bar, kept nearby specifically for this purpose, between the handles. She turned and surveyed the chapel.

It was empty.

"Anjelica?" she said aloud. "Honey?"

There was nothing but silence for a moment but then Mary Shelley heard a tiny, little girl whimper. She glanced at the barred door just as another burst of machine gun fire came from the hallway, followed quickly by another, louder, single blast. And then it was quiet again.

They were getting closer.

Mary Shelley ran from the door, up the aisle, past the pews and onto the chapel stage. She dropped behind the dark wooden podium there and pried open the small door in the back.

Anjelica cried out as the light hit her and began sobbing when she recognized Mary Shelley.

"It's okay, honey, we're okay," she said. "We're not going to let them get us."

"Who are they?" Anjelica whispered.

"I don't know," Mary Shelley said, and they both flinched as another eruption of machine gun fire clattered nearer than before, closer to the chapel doors, followed again by that single, louder blast.

A shotgun, Mary Shelley thought fearfully. *That sounds like a really big shotgun.*

"You stay in here, honey," Mary Shelley told Anjelica. "And don't come out. For anything. You'll be safe in here, I promise." She knew her promise was a good one. The podium had been reinforced five years ago with layers of steel and Kevlar so that it was completely and utterly bullet-proof.

"What about you?" Anjelica asked.

"I'll be fine," Mary Shelley told her. "Don't you worry about me."

The Reverend Mother closed the podium and raced back up the aisle to the main doors. She dove behind the last row of podiums just as a double rake of submachine gun fire burst out near the doors, followed swiftly by a double blast of that alarmingly loud and very final-sounding return fire.

For a few moments, there was complete silence. Mary Shelley stood slowly and crept cautiously on her tiptoes toward the double doors. She stood beside them, not wanting to make herself a target in case someone had the stupid idea of trying to shoot them down and put her ear flat against the wall.

She could hear people moving around out there, but there was no talking, no telling what they were up to.

Someone tried the doors. Of course, they were locked tight. Suddenly, something banged hard against them. Once, twice, three times. It was the sound of a heavy weapon being slammed against the door. Mary Shelley couldn't help but wince at each pounding but was confident the doors would hold.

"Reverend Mother," said the big voice of Simon Cadabra from the other side of the doors. "Unless you've got an army of nuns in there with you, then this is over." He gave a low chuckle. "And, by my count, you don't have any nuns left."

Mary Shelley hugged the wall behind the doors and held her MAC-11 at the ready.

"I'm going to give you to the count of ten," Cadabra said through the doors. "And then my friends and I are going to knock these doors down. And we're not going to be happy about all the extra work you've made us do to get inside. And we're probably gonna take that frustration out on you. So, just open the doors and we'll make it nice and easy on you. If you don't … well, let's just say it won't be very easy. It won't be very easy at all."

And then he began counting. "Ten. Nine. Eight." Loudly. Abrasively. *Even if he wasn't trying to kill me*, Mary Shelley thought, *I still wouldn't like this guy.*

"Seven. Six. Five."

Mary Shelley lifted her weapon, pressed close against the wall near the double doors.

"Four," Cadabra continued, slowing the countdown a bit as he got to three, two and finally, "One."

There was a moment of complete and utter silence.

"All right, Reverend Mother," Cadabra said at last. "If that's how you want to play it."

And Mary Shelley flinched violently as there was another roaring blast and the doors rattled in their frame and pieces flew off into the pews. Another blast, and more of the doors were ripped away. Mary Shelley envisioned the giant Cadabra standing on the other side, firing what must be a *huge* shotgun again and again into the wood there. A third blast, then a fourth. And the doors started to give way. A fifth blast and the left door sagged on its hinge. A moment later, a massive hand reached through and pulled the rest of the door out of the way.

Mary Shelley crouched beside the now ruined doors, weapon at the ready. She braced herself for what she knew was coming next.

But they were on her before she could react. The three homeless men, *dead* homeless men, suddenly surged through the ragged remains of the chapel doors and were on her almost instantly. She managed to get off a shot sewed a line of bullet holes across their midriffs, but still they came. They were on her, clawing at her, snatching the MAC-11 away and sending it sailing into the pews. Then they had control of her and held her as Cadabra stepped into the chapel, a monster of a man with a monster of a shotgun, the biggest Mary Shelley had ever seen, ridiculously, comically so, held at his side. Twin streams of smoke snaked from its matching barrels.

"Hello, Reverend Mother," Cadabra said. "Where's the girl?"

"She's not here!" Mary Shelley said. "She's gone. We took her away when we found out you were coming."

Cadabra smiled. "You didn't know we were coming," he said. "But nice try. Get her to her feet," he told his drones.

He stepped deeper into the chapel. "We know where she's not," he said. "We searched each of the rooms we came through and we had a few, um … conversations … with your friends out there." He stopped, turned around in the aisle and looked back at Mary Shelley. "Your *former* friends, I should say. Your *late* friends might be even more accurate."

He continued toward the stage. "So, we know she's in here," he said. "And there aren't a lot of hiding places in this room. So, we'll find her eventually, and I figured we'd let you watch."

"Go to Hell," Mary Shelley spat.

"That's the plan," Cadabra said. He stepped nimbly and somewhat eagerly, Mary Shelley noted, onto the stage. Her heart sputtered as she watched him peer behind curtains, open cabinets, even peek into vases where the girl couldn't possibly be hiding. Finally, he stepped onto the stage and walked directly to the podium, standing behind it as though poised to give a speech. Mary Shelley's heart stopped.

"You know, Reverend Mother, in fact there is only one place this wonderful girl could be hiding. And I believe that the two of us, you and I, know exactly where that is." He leaned down, groaning mildly with effort, and touched the latch on the podium. From inside came the slightest frightened whimper, and Mary Shelley could see Cadabra's smile of triumph all the way from the back of the chapel.

Her eyes were riveted on Cadabra and the podium, but peripherally Mary Shelley caught sight of sudden movement near the remnants of the chapel doors and she winced as a rapid triple blast of gunshots rang out and Cadabra's drones released their cold, stiff grips and fell away from her. She cried out and her hands jumped up to her face.

And suddenly, there was a man in the chapel with her, a man in a tan trench coat and a black fedora, and he was walking down the aisle, a handgun held out in front of him, pointing it directly at an obviously startled Cadabra.

Cadabra blinked. "Who the hell are you?" he asked, caught off guard.

"Richard Keane," the man replied. He pulled the trigger twice and put a matching set of black bullet holes right between Cadabra's wide-set eyes. "Private investigator."

Private Investigator Richard Keane felt a thrill of satisfaction as his slugs found their mark, punching two black holes into the giant head of the man at the podium. The giant fell back almost gracefully, his massive body dropping to the wooden stage floor with a thunderous boom. Keane had no regrets in filling the guy's head with lead. He'd seen the giant's cannon-like shotgun and he'd witnessed its messy handiwork on his way into the chapel.

A moment later, a nun rushed past him, snatched an MAC-11 from between pews (Keane had to admit that a nun with a gun was something he'd never expected to see) and ran to the stage. He followed her and watched as she yanked open the small door at the back of the podium and a young girl sprang out, clutching the nun in an explosive combination of horror and relief.

Keane had never seen her before but recognized her immediately.

Anjelica.

His assignment.

Keane watched the reunion for a moment or two, feeling wildly out of place and almost a little embarrassed at the thickness of emotion. Finally, without releasing her hold on the child, the nun looked up at him, tears of joy and despair running down her cheeks, and said, "Thank you."

"My pleasure," Keane said. He pointed the barrel of his weapon toward the body of the huge man lying dead on stage. "You have to shoot them in the head, you know? Just like on *The Walking Dead.*"

The nun stared back at him blankly.

"The name's Keane, by the way," he said, tucking his weapon into the holster beneath his arm and offering his hand. "Richard Keane."

Mary Shelley took it and he pulled her to her feet. She, in turn, tugged Anjelica to hers. "I'm Mother Superior Mary Shelley. And this ..."

"This is Anjelica," Keane said, holding out his hand again. "Young lady, I'm very pleased to meet you." He was surprised when the girl pulled away from the nun, took his hand, pumped it twice, and released it. Tears of fear were still drying on her cheeks but she seemed to have recovered quite nicely.

"I'm happy to meet you, too," she said pleasantly.

"How'd you know?" Mary Shelley asked. "How'd you know her name?"

"I know a lot of things, sister ..."

"*Mother Superior*," Mary Shelley corrected.

"Mother, Mom, whatever," Keane said. "We can talk about all that later. Right now, we gotta get the hell out of here."

"What? Where to?"

"My car's waiting just outside," Keane said.

Mary Shelley hesitated. Keane could sense her indecision. He knew she didn't know him from Adam and that she had to balance her trust in him with her dedication to protect the girl. "Honestly, lady, I'm on your side," he said. "But we gotta go. This guy might be down ..." He nodded again at the prostrate Cadabra. "…But you can bet they'll be sending more."

"Who are *they?*"

"*They* is all you need to know right now," Keane told her. Once again, he caught the look of concern on her features. "Look, I'm not trying to keep things from you, we just don't have the time to discuss it right now. Please trust me. I'm the good guy here. Let's go!"

They ran back through the aisle toward the devastated chapel doors and into the hallway. There, Keane stopped them. "You'd better carry her from here," he told Mary Shelley. "You don't want her to see this." And he was glad when the nun scooped up the girl and held her face to her shoulder, whispering, "Close your eyes, honey. Close your eyes."

They ran through the hallways and they dodged the carnage that littered the floor and splattered the walls. Keane could sense that Mary Shelley wanted to slow down, to say goodbye and perhaps offer a prayer for her fallen sisters, but he anxiously urged her on and finally they were out the front door and sprinting to a beautiful black 1969

Dodge Charger that gleamed in the afternoon daylight like a metal stallion awaiting its riders. Keane opened the passenger door and took Anjelica from Mary Shelley's reluctant arms. "You sit in the back," he told Anjelica, "And keep your head low."

He was pleased to see Anjelica following his orders exactly. He moved the front seat back into place and held the door for Mary Shelley. She stopped again and looked him in the eyes. "Where are we going?" she asked.

"Out of town," Keane told her. He nudged the MAC-11 hanging from its strap by her side. "Keep this close." As though encouraged by his acknowledgement of the weapon slung around her shoulders, Mary Shelley climbed in. Keane closed the door behind her, ran around to the driver's side, plunged the key into the slot on the steering column and brought the powerful V8 engine to life.

A moment later, they were on South 8th Street, Keane keeping the car at just enough past the speed limit so he wouldn't get pulled over. The last thing he needed now was to get pulled over for a speeding ticket, spattered with blood and with an eight-year old and a machine gun-carrying nun in the car with him. *Try to explain that,* he thought, *and the fact that there are a dozen dead bodies back at the convent.* They took a sharp left at Fremont and Keane edged the Charger on a little farther, racing up toward North Las Vegas Boulevard at the fastest yet smartest possible speed.

Keane sensed that the Reverend Mother was staring at him but was unwilling to take his eyes off the road. After a moment, he asked, "What?"

Mary Shelley flinched. "I'm sorry," she said quickly. "This has all been such a shock. I'm still a little over-whelmed by it all."

"That's completely understandable," Keane said. "I'll explain it all when we get a chance to breathe. Right now, we've got to get out of Vegas."

Traffic wasn't bad on this part of the Boulevard, far from where most of the tourist congestion was on the Southern side of the Strip, and Keane soon burned through a yellow light and onto an on-ramp, merging onto the US-95 North. The traffic was slow in the right lanes but, as Keane merged left, he was able to open the Charger up to an even 80, its engine purring in a throaty, satisfying roar.

"You seem to be enjoying this," Mary Shelley accused him, her brows furrowed in uncertainty.

Keane realized he'd been grinning. "It's my dream car," he said matter-of-factly. "Never thought I'd be driving one."

Mary Shelley shook her head in disbelief.

The Charger swung a wide left and Keane slipped off US-95 North and onto I-15 South. A sign reading "Speed Limit: 75" rose out of the fading sunlight and Keane pushed the Charger to 85. There were two options for a quick rest spot, he thought. There was Primm, about thirty minutes away, famous for its three hotel casinos for various budgets (in ascending order, Whiskey Pete's, Buffalo Bill's and Primm Valley Resort) and its popular outlet mall. Primm was also the home of the "Bonnie & Clyde Death Car," proclaimed to be the actual car that legendary bandits Bonnie & Clyde were gunned to death in. But, as much as Keane thought he wouldn't mind seeing that, Primm would be busy, as it always was, because it was the first cluster of casinos where the border of California met the border of Nevada. Not only did the tour buses stop there but so did hundreds of thousands of cars on their way to Sin City. It was the appetizer to Las Vegas' entrée.

The Gold Strike in Jean seemed a better choice. It was ten minutes closer than Primm and sometimes almost eerily empty. There was less chance of the wrong people seeing them there and, better yet, less chance of the wrong people *finding* them there. It would give them a moment for the bathroom and maybe a quick Coke and then they could be on their way to Stop #1: Baker, California.

"We're gonna stop up here in about fifteen minutes," Keane told Mary Shelley. "And I'll tell you everything I know." He gave a low chuckle. "You may want to brace yourself. Some of it's going to blow your mind."

"I look forward to it," Mary Shelley said, steely-eyed.

Keane saw a billboard reading "Stay at Jean! $34.95 a night!" and gave the Charger just a little more gas.

Chapter Fourteen

"Well, you sure screwed that up!"

Simon Cadabra awoke with a start, choking a little on what he hoped wasn't sleep drool, only to find himself sitting in one of the gray metal chairs in Clay Watkins' grim little office. His shoulders slumped when he discovered that he was no longer dead.

"Wasn't *all* your fault," Watkins continued, in an almost apologetic tone of voice that was really unlike him. "No one knew that Keane fellow was going to be there. Man, did he bust you up or what?" His skeletal hand came up and the pointy tip of a finger hovered just before Cadabra's face.

Cadabra reached up and touched the bridge of his nose, just between his two wide-set eyes. He could feel twin depressions there, round little holes now filled with scar tissue, and he suddenly remembered the double *blam-blam* of .45 caliber bullets boring into this skull.

"What happened?" he asked.

"Your assignment got side-swiped," Watkins said. "By the other guys. They sent a private dick ... a private *dick!* ... and he got to the girl before you did."

"God *dammit!*" Cadabra spat, striking his fist on the desktop. "I was so close!"

"You know where 'close' counts," Watkins said. "And it sure as hell ain't here."

"So now what?" Cadabra said. His face burned with a flush of anger. "That bastard shot me twice in the face. I want to nail that smug son of a bitch."

"Well, you'll get your chance," Watkins said. "Powers that be said to send you back up. You screwed the pooch this time round, but they decided to give you another go." He took a sip from the bottle of water on his desk and wiped his mouth with the sleeve of his white shirt. "We don't know where they are at the moment, but we know where they're going next. You're gonna meet them there."

"Where?" Cadabra said eagerly.

"Baker, California," Watkins told him and snickered like an old man watching a porno movie.

"What the hell do they want there?"

"We don't know," Watkins said. "Our intel only got us so much. But we know this: There are three of them: Keane, a nun, and the brat. They're heading to Baker, California. They're driving a black, 1969 Dodge Charger ..."

"What a cliché," Cadabra said with revulsion.

Watkins shrugged.

"Okay," Cadabra said. "When do I go back?"

"As soon as you come up with a plan," Watkins said. "But the clock is ticking."

Cadabra felt an ugly grin creep onto his face and latch on there like a black widow spider upon its prey. "Oh, I'll come up with something," he said.

Keane was glad that Anjelica, who had lain in the back seat silently since they had left the convent, was sitting up and seemed actually excited about the Gold Strike. Maybe it was the glittering lights and giant electric signs that flashed brightly, even in the still blazing late afternoon sun. Maybe it was the Western movie style of the casino's multi-colored design, complete with signs reading "Wild Rose Saloon," "Bank" and (probably of most interest to Anjelica) "Ice Cream." An enormous thousand-bulbed marquee at the front of the casino alternately flashed "Surf & Turf Buffet: $11.99 (11pm – 6am only)" and "5x Odds on Roulette."

Keane slowed the Charger, pulled into the left turn lane and waited while a veritable parade of traffic, most of them driving entirely too fast in a hurry to get to Las Vegas, rushed past them. When a break finally came, Keane punched it and the Charger leapt across the three lanes of opposing traffic and into the Gold Strike parking lot.

As Keane had expected, the lot wasn't very full. There were maybe a dozen cars in the parking lot at best, and a half dozen more parked in the upper rear corner behind a sign that read EMPLOYEE PARKING. The gravelly blacktop crunched as Keane pulled the Charger around to the rear of the casino so it wouldn't be seen from the bustling freeway out front.

They sat for a moment in silence as Keane killed the engine. After a moment, Anjelica said, "Are we going to get out?"

Keane looked at her reflection in the rearview mirror. "You saw that Ice Cream sign, didn't you?"

Anjelica nodded, her eyes brightening.

"You like chocolate, vanilla or strawberry?" Keane asked.

"Peanut butter!" Anjelica proclaimed.

"Peanut butter?" Keane protested playfully. "Oh, all right. Let's go get some ice cream." He grabbed his fedora from the dashboard, slipped it on, opened the door and climbed out, pushing his chair forward and letting Anjelica clamber over it.

"You've got a hole in your hat," Anjelica said, pointing.

"Yes, I do, Anjelica," Keane said. "Yes, I do."

Mary Shelley got out on her side and together they went in.

Like all Las Vegas style casinos, the interior of the Gold Strike was gaudy and beautiful all at once. The vaulted ceilings were festooned with saloon-inspired lighting and hidden security cameras. The carpet was a mishmash of red and gold swirls. The electronic tinkling of slot machines filled the air and occasionally the sound of coins falling into a tray broke through it all (although one could never be certain whether there were actual coins or just a tinny recording).

Keane scanned the casino floor. There was a handful of patrons plying the slot machines for big wins and only one of the tables was open, for a game called "Let It Ride." A grim-faced man wearing a full beard, compression leggings and a tattered pair of sandals sat there, nursing what looked like a watered-down Jack and Coke. *Seems normal enough,* Keane thought. He located the ice cream shop and was relieved to see it was right next door to the diner. He pulled out his wallet and fished out a few dollar bills. "Hey, Anjelica. Here's ten bucks. Go big."

The girl laughed with delight, snatched the bills out of Keane's hand and ran straight to the ice cream shop. Keane and Mary Shelley both smiled broadly as they watched her go.

"An hour ago," Keane said, "She was scared to death that someone was coming to kill her. Now she wants ice cream."

"She's an amazing kid," Mary Shelley said.

"Most of them are," Keane agreed. "Why don't we get a cup of coffee," he said, nodding toward the diner, "and talk a little about what's going on."

"I think that's a good idea."

** ** **

The server in the white suit and silly hat told her they didn't have plain peanut butter ice cream, so Anjelica had to get chocolate peanut butter crunch instead. She was glad she did. The ice cream was the very best she'd had in a long time and the "crunch" bits seemed to be some kind of sweet cereal—like Cap'n Crunch Peanut Butter maybe.

She'd gone back to the table where the grown-ups were talking and the man, Mr. Keane, had given her a few more dollars to play in the arcade on the other side of the diner. Anjelica was thrilled. She didn't get to play many video games at the convent (despite the fact that Sister Cecelia had an Xbox 360) because Reverend Mother said video-games were too violent.

Anjelica's shoulders drooped. She missed Sister Cecelia. And she had a feeling she wouldn't ever see her again.

She stepped into the arcade and glanced around at all the different videogames available to play there. She saw Pac-Man of course, and a game called Galaga and another called Asteroids. Asteroids didn't look like much fun because it was all black-and-white. Anjelica preferred full color.

She glanced back at the adults and watched them for a moment. They appeared to be having some kind of deep conversation. Mr. Keane was nodding his head emphatically and thumping his finger on the table and Reverend Mother was shaking her head and wagging her finger.

Anjelica was glad she was in the arcade.

** ** **

Keane took a sip of his coffee and was surprised once again at how hot and how weak it was. Back in the day, coffee was hot but didn't burn a hole in your tongue. And it had *flavor*. This was almost like weak tea. No big deal. He wasn't really a coffee drinker, anyway. His beverage of choice was Coca-Cola and, to his taste at least, it hadn't changed much in sixty years.

He glanced over at Reverend Mother Mary Shelley, sitting across the Formica table from him, sipping her coffee and apparently having no complaints about it. "Okay," he said. "You go first."

"I'd rather you did," she said. "You seem to know a little more about me than I know about you."

Keane gave her a look that said he disagreed.

"You knew where to find me," Mary Shelley explained. "And all I know about you is that you drive an old Charger."

"Actually, I knew where to find *her*," Keane said, nodding in Anjelica's direction. "But I get your point. So here goes: I am a private detective from Los Angeles. I was born in 1921 and I was killed by a gunman in 1954." He touched the hole in the side of his hat. "I've spent the past sixty years in a place called Betwixt, which is something like Purgatory with a different name. Recently, a fat little baby with hummingbird wings came to me and told me I had a mission: to transport a little girl from Las Vegas to Santa Barbara and to protect her from any harm. If I succeed, I get to move onto the next plane, whatever the hell that is. They sent me back to Earth to complete my assignment and now here I am, sitting in a casino across from a nun with a machine gun." He took a sip of his coffee and stared back into Mary Shelley's stunned, slack-jawed face. "Okay," he said. "Now you go."

** ** **

Anjelica made a full circle of the relatively small room, around the air hockey table and the claw machines. She wandered around the arcade until she saw a game that scared her and thrilled her at the same time.

It was called "Demon's World." And, as though it had been waiting for her, there was a small wooden box on the floor in front of it, so even she could climb up and play.

** ** **

Mary Shelley reached for her coffee and nearly knocked the Styrofoam cup over because her hand was shaking so badly.

"So," Keane said. "I'm sure you think I'm crazy."

"Actually," Mary Shelley said, blowing on her coffee to cool it. "I'm more uncertain of my own sanity. Because … I believe you."

"You do?" Keane asked, astonished.

"I do," Mary Shelley continued. "Because it all ties in with what they told us."

"Who's 'they'?"

Mary Shelley laughed quietly. "Oh," she said. "Now *you're* asking that question."

Keane smiled and nodded. "I guess I am."

"Four years ago," Mary Shelley said. "A group of men brought Anjelica to the convent. They didn't identify themselves; they didn't say who they worked for. They just showed up one day at the front door. I could sense that they were military of some kind but, again, they never confirmed that."

"Mercenaries?" Keane asked.

"Maybe," Mary Shelley said. "They had paperwork confirming they were on assignment for The Vatican and that they would be spending the next three months with us. We were beside ourselves. Not only did we have a child to care for, we now had *tenants*." She took a sip of her coffee, added a bit more creamer from the jar of powder on the table. "In the three months that followed, however, we discovered that they were much more than tenants ... they were instructors. They taught us how to defend ourselves, both in hand-to-hand combat and with weapons they provided. And, at the end of that three months, they gave us our orders: Protect the little girl, protect Anjelica, at all costs. Her safety was of paramount importance."

"So that's how you learned to use a machine gun," Keane said.

Mary Shelley nodded.

"Why didn't they just leave the mercs there?" Keane asked. "Why go to all the trouble training you?"

"I asked that question," Mary Shelley said. "The answer I got is that they wanted to draw as little attention as possible as to Anjelica's whereabouts. They told me that she was in terrible danger and that, someday, someone would try to take her. They had trained us to be ready when that day came."

"And now that day has come," Keane said. He reached for his coffee, glanced over in Anjelica's direction, and froze. A split second later, he was out of his seat and racing for the arcade.

** ** **

Anjelica stepped up on the box, dug out one of the quarters she'd changed for her dollar bills, and inserted it into the slot marked "Deposit Coin(s)." Immediately, the machine began to chirp in that annoying, electronic music that Anjelica and kids around the world found delightful.

Her game began. After asking her for her initials (Anjelica entered AAA), her character appeared: A squat square-headed man with orange hair, wearing a blue jump suit, dark glasses and carrying a gun that looked like something a spy would carry but fired energy pulses like the Ghostbusters. As Anjelica guided her character to the right, he was met by impish demons of various sizes and colors and he blew them away with bursts of electricity that turned them either into miniature nuclear clouds or fiery red orbs.

Anjelica was so engrossed in destroying demons that she only once looked over her shoulders for the grown-ups, who were still deep in heavy conversation, and she didn't even hear the man walk up behind her until he said, "Excuse me, miss, but I need you to come with me."

Her blood froze and she felt the hackles on her neck rise up. She wanted to scream but she was afraid if she did the man would try to hurt her, like those men back at the convent. So instead, she let go of the game controls (her character quickly died a fiery and apparently painful death) and stepped down off the box. The man reached down for her with a massive, hairy hand and Anjelica reluctantly reached up and took it.

And then Mr. Keane was there, with a wild-eyed Reverend Mother standing behind him. Mr. Keane stood directly in front of the other man so he couldn't get by. Anjelica saw that Mr. Keane's hand was inside his jacket and she wondered why he was walking around like that. Did his chest hurt?

"Do we have a problem here?" Mr. Keane asked, and the tone of his voice even made Anjelica a little afraid.

The other man stood a little straighter but was still at least a few inches shorter than Mr. Keane. "Not at all," the man said. "Hotel security. The girl can't be in the arcade on her own. Has to be with someone 17 or older."

"Oh, thanks," Mr. Keane said, and Anjelica could see his shoulders relax and an apologetic smile appear on his face. "Sorry. Didn't know there were rules."

"She's welcome to play as long as you're in the arcade with her," the security guard said pleasantly. "For her own safety, you understand."

"Of course," Mr. Keane said. "My apologies. Come on, Anjelica. It's time to get going anyway."

The security guard released Anjelica's hand (she was glad to be free of his warm clammy fingers) and she reached up to take Mr. Keane's.

"I'm sorry, Mr. Keane," she said.

"No need to be," Keane told her. "You did nothing wrong. Did you finish your ice cream?"

"No!" Anjelica dropped his hand and ran back to get her cup of ice cream, still sitting on the Demon Hunter machine. It was a little runny now, but it still tasted good. Ice cream was ice cream!

She hopped back and joined the grown-ups, taking Mr. Keane's hand again, and together they exited the Gold Strike Hotel & Casino.

The only lights on the road from Jean to Baker were whatever spilled over from the billboards and the headlights and taillights of other cars speeding to and fro. The freeway here meandered over hills and through valleys in a manner that made it impossible to discern one mile from another. It seemed like an endless procession of dull ups and downs.

Keane kept the Charger at 85, despite the speed limit changing from 75 to 70, and they were at the top of the long grade that declined slowly from the last hill to the valley ahead. A sign post announced "Baker, 10 miles" and Mary Shelley could see the lights of the tiny city in the distance. It made her uneasy and she decided that this was the time to ask some additional pertinent questions. "Why are we stopping here?" she asked.

"I told you, I don't know," Keane said. "My instructions were simply to get Anjelica safely from Las Vegas to

Santa Barbara, and to stop at these four locations on the way."

He handed her a yellow notepad page divided with faint blue lines. A numbered list of destinations was printed in ballpoint thereon.

"But why?" Mary Shelley asked again. "I mean, it doesn't make any sense." She unconsciously dropped her hand down between the seat and the door where the MAC-11 languished. Its cool metal surface was strangely comforting to her.

"Yeah," Anjelica said from the back seat. "Why?"

"See, that's what worries me," Keane said to the girl. "They told me *you're* supposed to know."

An incredulous look shadowed Mary Shelley's face as she realized Keane was talking to Anjelica. "*She's* supposed to know? She's supposed to know *what?*"

"I don't know anything!" Anjelica cried.

"You keep asking the same questions," Keane said. "And I have to keep giving you the same answer. I don't know."

"So maybe we don't have to stop," Mary Shelley said, warming to the idea. "Maybe we can just go on through. Drive straight through to Santa Barbara. Wouldn't that be safer anyway?"

"I don't know," Keane said. "They must want us to stop at these places for a reason."

"What reason?"

"*I don't know!*"

The town of Baker grew larger in the windshield before them. It was a small town, really, perhaps only a dozen small buildings or so. Mary Shelley had stopped there often in the past, on road trips to L.A. and back, and knew the area well. There was a casual dining restaurant there (once called, amusingly, "Bun Boy,"), a liquor store famous for winning lottery tickets, a shop advertising "Alien Jerky" and a Greek restaurant that was reported to have "the largest menu in California," sporting everything from Gyros to deep fried burritos to grilled cheese sandwiches.

Oh and, of course, there was the World's Tallest Thermometer.

But what did any of these things have to do with Anjelica? What could a little seven year old girl do for anybody or anything in a desert city best known for its date shakes and a towering gauge whose sole purpose was to remind you that the desert is hotter than hell? What did anything in Baker ... or Calico or Vasquez Rocks or any of the places Keane had been ordered to stop at ... have to do with a little girl?

Another sign solidified in the dark night air. "Baker. Next right." Mary Shelley could see the northern end of town now, could make out a Del Taco sign and what looked like an Arby's restaurant/gas station combo. She could see the 134-foot thermometer up ahead, only about half its lights working, the rest either burned out or too filthy to shine through. The temperature read somewhere in the low 100s, but she couldn't be certain because most of the reading's lights were burned out too and instead of "103" it looked like "LC&" or something. She tried to remember the last time she'd seen the thermometer working properly and realized she could not.

Beside her, Keane was having second thoughts of his own. *Maybe I won't stop*, he thought. *What's the worst that can happen? Maybe I'll just zip by Baker and then Lake Dolores. I'll skip Calico and drive straight through Mojave and, as much as I love the beauty of Vasquez Rocks, I can see that just fine from the freeway, thank you, and I'll get to Santa Barbara an hour or two early. Really? What's the harm in that?*

But he knew that Buster had told him to stop for a reason and, even though that "reason" had apparently been above Keane's pay grade, he wasn't about to take chances on an assignment that could get him out of his tiny office floating in the middle of space. So, he tapped the blinker with his left hand and heard it start to *clack clack clack* as the red indicator on the dash made the cabin glow red, then go black, then red, then black.

"So, you're gonna stop?" Mary Shelley said with venom.

"I think we have to," Keane said.

"I don't want to!" Anjelica cried, and threw herself back in the seat, arms crossed tightly across her chest, her face defiant.

"Don't you want to see the world's tallest thermometer?" Keane asked, cooing to Anjelica in the back seat. "It's in the Guinness Book of World Records! One hundred and thirty-four feet. That's over ten stories tall! Don't you want to see that, Anjelica?"

And he felt a swelling of triumph as Anjelica uncrossed her arms and began to peer through the windows, trying to catch sight of it.

"We'll stop at the thermometer," Keane told Mary Shelley, "Pop out for a quick look, and then be on our way. Won't be five minutes. Okay?"

"If that's what you think is right," Mary Shelley said, but now her arms were crossed over her chest.

"Won't be five minutes," Keane said again, following the main road to the Del Taco parking lot that baked in the desert heat beside the half-lit thermometer. He pulled in and parked three stalls down from a dusty white Ford Econoline van, one of only three other cars in the lot.

** ** **

The stench of squirming demons was making Simon Cadabra's eyes water. It was a scent not unlike that of

132

smoldering sulfur combined with the body odor of over-worked longshoremen. And it burned the lining of his re-belling nostrils as though somebody had grabbed him by the ankles, held his body upside down and poured battery acid into his nose.

Still, he needed them, and it was the price he had to pay for their assistance. He turned the page on last month's *Mugshots Cavalcade Magazine* and pretended not to notice when the black '69 Dodge Charger pulled into the lot and parked a couple of spaces down. He watched out of the corner of his eyes as the Charger's window rolled down to reveal private investigator Richard Keane snatching his fe-dora from the dashboard and placing it on his head.

Oh, you smug son of a bitch, Cadabra thought, turning from the DUI page of the June *Mugshot* to the Check Fraud page. *I am so going to bring you down.*

"Is that them, Master?" said an oily voice beside Ca-dabra's ear. He turned to find the beefy, beet-red head of one of the five demons in the back of the van, peering out over his shoulder and staring at the Charger, the twin spiked horns on its head glistening in the bright parking lot lights.

"Get back there and stay down!" Cadabra spat, batting at the demon with his magazine. "I'll call you when I need you!"

"Yes, Master, sorry, Master," said the demon, slithering away into the back of the van.

Cadabra waited until he was sure the demon was settled again and then flipped the page, pretending to read about petty theft while carefully watching the Charger and its occupants.

We'll wait until all three of them are out of the car, Cadabra thought. *And then we'll take them all at once.*

** ** **

Keane popped open the driver's side door and stepped onto the asphalt. Even at this time of night, just before 6:30pm, he could feel the heat rising up into the sole of his shoe, through his sock, warming his foot. He allowed himself a luxurious stretch and then took a cautious look around.

The dinner hour appeared to be over and the Del Taco parking lot contained only two small sedans and a white van. The sedans appeared to be empty, their occupants probably inside enjoying a Macho Combo Burrito, and the driver of the van was busy reading some small edition newspaper, his baseball cap pulled down tightly over his skull. Keane gave him another look and decided he posed no threat. He flicked his wrist at the two passengers still in the Charger.

"C'mon out," he said.

The passenger door clicked open and Reverend Mother Mary Shelley got out, allowing herself a quick stretch before folding the seat forward, reaching in and helping Anjelica climb out of the back. Anjelica did her own miniature version of the long drive stretch and Keane watched her eyes with delight as they took in all 134 feet of the World's Tallest Thermometer. Her mouth fell open in a soft "O".

"That's it!" Keane announced regally. "The World's Tallest Thermometer."

It was ringed by a chain link fence and it rose up like a bargain basement presidential monument from a brown grass lot right next to Del Taco. Its four sides were each nearly eight feet across. Near the bottom of each side was a red circle with the words "Baker, CA. Gateway to Death Valley" emblazoned on it in white. Rising up from those words were eleven black ovals, one atop the other, coming to a peak near the top where two smaller dark squares (*Windows?* Keane wondered) marked the highest point.

The lowest black circle was lit with a neon "30" and the one above that read "40." The rest of the numbers, rising up to the second from the top, were illegible due to burned out lights, desert dust and crusty bird poop. The remaining ovals were completely dark, either because the temperature hadn't reached those heights or because they were burned out completely. Keane had read that the thermometer often didn't work and now he had seen it with his own eyes.

Still, he, Mary Shelley and Anjelica walked slowly over to the chain link fence and stared up at the strange monument with a mixture of awe, revulsion, and pity. *It's not every day*, Keane thought, *that you get to see the World's Tallest Thermometer.*

** ** **

Simon Cadabra added rotting garbage to the list of things that demons smelled like. The five in the back of his van, ranging in size from two feet to three and a half feet long, had all placed their heads between the van's front seats and they were panting heavily, almost in unison, excited at the nearness of their prey. Cadabra could smell their fecal breath and hear their sighing pants and a wave of disgust rolled through him.

"Now, Master?" one of the smaller demons hissed, its voice husky with impatience.

"Wait," Cadabra said, folding his *Mugshot Magazine* and placing it on the passenger seat beside him. The demons mewed and whined and Cadabra snatched up the magazine and slapped it on the dashboard. "I said *wait!*" he spat. "Now be quiet!"

As the demons reluctantly began to calm down, Cadabra thought of the conversation he'd had with Watkins earlier:

"Baker, California," Watkins had told him.

"What the hell do they want there?"

"We don't know," Watkins said. "Our intel only got us so much."

Cadabra watched the three targets walk away from the Charger and over to the fence surrounding the thermometer. *Maybe this is our chance*, he thought. *Maybe this is our chance to find out what they're up to. Get the intel we need.* Not that he could care less about that information personally, but it would be a nice feather in his cap and another step closer to getting out of The Office. He removed his baseball cap and pushed his thick-lensed glasses up closer to his eyes and he watched. There would be plenty of time to do what needed to be done with the girl. For now, he decided to just observe.

** ** **

"Is there a point to this?" Mary Shelley said impatiently. "Big thermometer, so what?" She waited a moment and was irritated by Keane's lack of a reply. "Look, you said five minutes, we gave you five minutes. Let's get back on the road."

"But, Reverend Mother," Anjelica said beside her, and Mary Shelley looked down to see the girl's eyes wide with wonder, her smile lighting up with childish awe. "It's so beautiful," Anjelica said simply.

"It is," Keane agreed. "But Reverend Mother is right. We've got to get going."

Mary Shelley watched with relief as Keane took Anjelica's hand and led her back to the car. As she walked behind them, she glanced over at the white van parked nearby and, in particular, the man in the driver's seat. For a reason she couldn't explain, she realized there was something about it she didn't like.

It probably had something to do with that butt ugly dog in the man's lap ...

** ** **

The demons were close to rebellion now and Cadabra realized with disgust that they were drooling heavily on the rubber matted floor. Their syrupy, yellow saliva reeked of rotten eggs.

"Now, Master?" one of them said, and began creeping across Cadabra's lap. He smacked at its head with the back

139

of his hand, scratching his knuckles on its left horn, and cursed.

"Get in the back, dammit!" he cried. "I think she saw you!"

The demons reluctantly retreated and Cadabra watched with dawning horror as the three targets climbed back into the Charger and its engine roared to gas-guzzling life.

"You're letting them get away!" a demon mewed miserably as the Charger pulled onto the main road and headed for the freeway entrance.

"They're not getting away," Cadabra said as much to himself as to the angry demons. "We'll catch up with them at the next stop."

"Why we wait?" said another demon, its yellow-pink eyes blinking in confusion.

"I wanted to see what they were up to," Cadabra explained, again as much to himself as the demons. "I wanted to see what they did."

"They got out and looked at the big broken thing," another demon cackled, and the rest of the demons fell about themselves, kicking their legs and holding their bellies and laughing hysterically like rabid jackals.

What were they doing here? Cadabra thought, ignoring the demons' helpless orgy of laughter. *And what are they supposed to do at their next three stops?*

After a moment, he started the van, yelled at the demons to shut the hell up, and pulled onto the main road. A few seconds later, they were on the Interstate 15, heading toward Lake Dolores.

Behind them, the World's Tallest Thermometer—its every light suddenly shining brightly, its every temperature reading completely legible, its every bulb looking like it was out-of-the-box brand new and shiny clean—shone like a crimson beacon in the middle of the desert, telling the world that the temperature here was a perfect, pleasant 80 degrees.

It had been known by many names throughout the years—The Lake Dolores Waterpark; Rock-a-Hoola Waterpark; Discovery Waterpark—and it had brought joy and fun to tens of thousands of visitors. Its winding Lazy River had been a favorite attraction for avoiding the prickly summer heat, as were the multitudinous waterslides and swimming pools.

But now the park sat in desolate ruins, like something out of an apocalyptic sci-fi movie. Its majestic waterslides were gone, either rotten and dilapidated or dismantled and shipped off to other, still living, parks. The buildings, once sporting brightly painted signs announcing ARCADE or GIFTS or LAZY RIVER CAFÉ, were now no more than crumbling walls, so heavily laden with graffiti it was impossible to see even a spot of the original color. The pathways were lousy with litter and debris and even the palm trees looked dead and gray.

Interstate 15 buzzed frenetically just a hundred feet away and yet seemed to be from a different world than the remains of what was once a place filled with sun-drenched tourists and laughing, playful children.

In the darkness, Keane had actually passed the park and had to get off at the next exit, taking a bridge over the freeway and returning from the opposite direction. Reverend Mother Mary Shelley, who had been almost silent since they had left Baker about forty minutes ago, made a brief, snide remark about wasting time, but didn't press the issue.

"Where are we going now?" Anjelica asked from the back seat.

"A waterpark," Keane told her.

"A waterpark!" Anjelica said, leaning forward and stretching her seatbelt to its full length.

"Don't get your hopes up," Keane told her. "It's an old waterpark. Been closed for years. There are no more waterslides, hell, there's not even any more water!"

"Then why are we going?" Anjelica groused, falling back into the seat.

Keane smiled. "As if you would want to go in the water at this time of night, anyway," he teased.

"I would!" Anjelica said.

Keane shook his head. "I don't believe it," he said.

"She would," Mary Shelley said beside him. "That one loves the water."

Keane got off the freeway, turned left and took another bridge across it. He drove in darkness for a few minutes—the only light that of the Charger's headlights and the dim glow of the nearby freeway—until they arrived at the front gate of the waterpark and stopped the car.

"Welcome to Rock-A-Hoola Waterpark," Anjelica read from a peeling billboard nearby. She peered at what ruins and debris she could see through the chain link fence surrounding the property and pouted. "This place makes me sad."

"Me, too," Keane agreed. "Excuse me," he said to Mary Shelley, and then reached down by her knees and opened the glovebox. He removed a large flashlight and closed the door. "Let's go take a look." He nodded at the

MAC-11 now sitting in Mary Shelley's lap. "Bring that," he whispered.

They got out of the car and walked to the main gate, their feet crunching loudly on the dry gravel. The gate, too, was made out of chain link, and someone had conveniently slit it open from top to bottom, apparently with a pair of bolt cutters. Keane peeled it back like a shower curtain and nodded. "After you," he said, and Mary Shelley and Anjelica stepped through.

Up close, the sight was even grimmer. Not only did graffiti cover everything in what seemed like three layers deep, it appeared that every window was broken, every door hung off its hinge. There was so much litter and debris along the pathways that Keane began to wonder if a landfill were nearby. What was left of the water attractions was broken and discarded and the concrete groove that made up the once popular Lazy River was cracked and shattered into blocky cement rocks almost every step of the way.

"This place makes me sad," Anjelica said again.

"Okay, Supersleuth," Mary Shelley said. "Now what?"

Keane shrugged in frustration. "Your guess is as good as mine," he said.

"You saw what happened back at Baker, didn't you?"

Keane knew the answer she was hunting for but shook his head.

"That's right," Mary Shelley added. "Because nothing did. We've got to stop wasting our time like this. Those men could be right behind us."

"I'm just following instructions," Keane told her. He wished Buster were here to explain it. But then Buster claimed he didn't know either.

"Your instructions may get us all killed."

"Look, dammit" Keane said, a little more harshly than he intended. He glanced past Mary Shelley's shocked glare, and saw Anjelica a short distance away, eyeing what had once been a spring-based rocking horse. He lowered his voice. "Look. I died in 1954. I got shot in the head right here." He touched the hole in his fedora, stuck his finger through, wiggled it. "And I died. And then, for some reason, I sat in a 200 square foot office for sixty damn years waiting for something to happen. And now it has. Now I'm here, in 2015, alive, back on Earth, and in charge of protecting an adorable and reportedly important little girl." He paused, took a deep breath, got hold of himself. "If you think I'm going to disobey whatever force put me back here, you are sadly mistaken, Reverend Mother. I'm not taking any chances with my future, or hers ..."

"Reverend Mother!" Anjelica cried, her voice full of girlish joy. "Mr. Keane! Look!"

Keane let his voice trail off as he and Mary Shelley turned to look. The hint of a smile tugged at the corners of Keane's mouth and he saw Mary Shelley was smiling, too.

Anjelica sat on the back of a large plastic frog, a huge metal spring stuck in the ground beneath it. She rocked back and forth on a saddle formed into the frog's back, the spring squeaking and creaking and sproinging, and her delightful little girl laugh twinkled across the desolate park like a fresh spring rain after a decade's worth of drought.

Keane felt his smile widen, and then became a quiet laugh. A moment later, Mary Shelley joined him, and they were laughing and cheering as Anjelica swung back and forth on the frog, giggling, and screaming and having a grand time.

And then there was a flash of movement from behind her and, by the time Keane had unleashed Whisper and Mary Shelley had brought up her MAC-11, the big man with the thick glasses—the man Keane had shot twice *in the face*—had snatched Anjelica off the plastic frog, tucked her under his left arm, and raised his own weapon with his right, the same behemoth shotgun that Keane had seen before, its wide-mouthed barrel pointed menacingly in their direction.

"Lower your weapons," he said with a sneer. "Or I'll crush her like a bug."

Keane thought about trying a shot anyway. The man was *huge*, six foot five if he was an inch, and Keane guessed well over 320 pounds. There was a lot more of him to target than there was of Anjelica, who squirmed ineffectively beneath the man's arm. Keane wasn't even sure the man could aim his shotgun properly one-handed, but he decided it wasn't worth it to take the chance.

He wasn't even sure if the man was here alone or had back up.

So, he lowered his weapon. After a moment, Mary Shelley lowered her MAC-11 as well.

"Very good," said the man.

"Who are you?" Keane asked.

"Ah," said the man, in a voice just as bold and as strong as his body size would indicate. "The very same question I asked you before you found it necessary to shoot me in the face."

"Twice," said Keane. "And good grouping, if I do say so myself. And, if I remember correctly, I did introduce myself first."

"Yes," said the man, smiling without humor. "I know who you are, Mr. Keane. Not only did you introduce yourself at our last meeting, but I have since been briefed on you. I know who you are, I know about your assignment, and I know where you are going." He paused as the girl squirmed again and he tightened his hold on her. "But what I don't know is what you're doing *here*. Or what you did back in Baker. Or what you're supposed to do on your remaining two stops."

"Welcome to the club," Keane said. "I don't know either."

"I guess that makes it my turn," the man said. He gave a short little bow. "My name is Simon Cadabra. I'm a Las Vegas magician who met, shall we say, an *untimely* death back in 2008."

"I know you," Mary Shelley interjected. "I remember when that happened. Saw it on the news! You burned to death on stage when a trick didn't go right."

Cadabra gave an ironic laugh. "It did make me rather famous," he said. "A little late, of course."

"So why are you here now?" Keane asked, making a note to get the rest of the story from Mary Shelley later. "Why are you following us?"

Cadabra seemed surprised. "Well, I would have thought that was obvious, Mr. Keane," he said. "The girl is *my* mission, too. Although, I expect our missions have completely different expected outcomes."

Keane knew exactly what Cadabra was saying. If Keane's mission was to save the girl, then Cadabra's was to stop her ... or kill her. He thought again about putting a couple of new holes in Cadabra but the risk was too great. But he had to do something.

"So, here's what we're going to do," Cadabra said, interrupting Keane's thoughts. "I'm going to take dear Anjelica here with me so she and I can discuss what it is she's supposed to accomplish on this journey of yours. *Her mission*, I'm going to call it. In the meantime, allow me to introduce you to my little friends."

Scarface, Keane thought. *1983. Al Pacino. Brian DePalma.*

And then there were things charging them from the shadows. Four of them, he counted, no, five! Small things, fast things, red things. Racing toward Keane and Mary Shelley like mad dogs with human faces, their teeth flashing and their razor-sharp nails digging ruts in the littered dirt.

Demons! And, oh, how they *stank!*

Keane lifted Whisper and shot the closest one point-blank in the face. It mewled in agony and rolled over onto its back, its arms and legs curling up beneath it like a dying spider, and then went still. He heard the rip of Mary Shelley's MAC-11, saw its line of bullets tear a hole through another demon's chest. "No!" He screamed. "The head! Shoot them in the head!" A bolt of pain shot through his ankle and he looked down to see another demon sinking its curved needle teeth deep into his shiny black shoe, spots of blood already squirting out of the puncture holes there. He lifted his other foot and drove it down on the demon's head, once, twice, a third time, and the demon's skull collapsed and its triangular head flattened beneath Keane's sole, a thick gray-ish fluid oozing out of its pointed ears like rancid oatmeal.

There was another burst from the MAC-11 and Keane saw a demon rip apart in mid-air as it leapt at Mary Shelley and she took Keane's advice and shot it through the eyes. Then something slammed into him at chest level and Keane went down, both pistol and fedora flying. He fell hard on his back, feeling rocks and sticks and rubble digging into him, and found himself face-to-face with a screeching demon, its forked tongue licking out behind its forest of serrated three-inch teeth, its rotten egg drool streaming out of both corners of its furious mouth.

Keane got his hands around its throat and squeezed. But it was no good. The demon was nothing but muscle and rage. Keane's strong grip wasn't enough to do any harm. The demon edged closer, baring its teeth, stretching its neck and reaching for Keane's throat. Its rancid breath brushed at Keane's cheeks.

Keane let go of the thing's throat with his right hand, keeping his left hand, his good hand, pressed into the meat of its neck. His right hand crabbed the ground, searching for a weapon but found nothing of use: a small rock, a crushed cardboard cup, a rotting newspaper, dried to a crisp from days, perhaps years, in the sun.

And then his fingertips touched something hard and round. He rolled it closer and managed to get a grip on it.

A short piece of white ¼" PVC piping, once carrying water to or from a nearby pool, about the length of a ruler and filthy from years of exposure, one end broken off to a sharp point. *Just what the doctor ordered.*

Keane gripped the PVC like a knife and quickly drove it into the demon's skull, just below the eye socket, and twisted it in until only about four inches remained. The demon screamed in pain and fury and then collapsed, its teeth raking Keane's cheek and leaving three lines of blood streaming down toward his chin.

He rolled the dead demon off him and got to his feet. Counting his most recent assailant, there were four dead demons splayed on the ground nearby him, which meant one was still out there. He was sure he had counted five!

Cadabra was gone and with him, Anjelica. Mary Shelley was nowhere to be seen.

Keane found his gun and his fedora and put them back where they belonged. He stood a moment, listening intently, but there was nothing but silence and the muffled sound of the nearby freeway. He wandered around briefly but could see nothing in the darkness and his short recon revealed nothing. His shoulders slumped. His foot and cheek throbbed. He sighed. Suddenly, just like that, it seemed that all was lost. He fell back against a sagging wall and slid down to a sitting position.

There was a soft pop and a white glow suddenly flared beside him. Keane, startled, looked up to find Buster hovering there, his plump little infant body held aloft by his busily beating cherub wings. "Hey, bub," Buster said. "Why the long face?"

Keane couldn't help but laugh. "Are you serious?" he asked between chuckles. "Or are you making a joke at my expense? I lost her, Buster. She's gone. And so is that nun who was with me. I lost them. I lost them both!"

"It's not over yet," Buster said.

"Of course, it is!"

"It is not," Buster continued. "Anjelica has done something unexpected that will perhaps save her life."

Keane couldn't help but be intrigued. "Oh? And what is that?"

"She's ignited Cadabra's curiosity," Buster said. "She's made him wonder about her purpose here."

"So?"

"So, if he planned on just killing her, he already would have. How many opportunities has he had in the past few hours?"

"Don't remind me."

"And yet, she lives. Why do you think that is?"

Keane pondered for a moment. *Buster makes a good point*, he thought. *Cadabra had ample opportunity to put a bullet in Anjelica's head just now, so why didn't he? What was it he had said just before the demons attacked?*

He was going to find out about her mission!

"So, he's taking her to the next stop!" Keane said, excitedly. "He wants to find out what she's supposed to be doing!"

"Hence," Buster said spreading his hands out, palms up. "It is not over."

"No," Keane said, standing with new purpose. "It most certainly is not."

Another soft pop and Buster was gone.

And Keane ran to the front gate, slipped through the slit in the chain link fence, raced to the Charger and dove in. In just a few moments he was roaring down the Interstate 15 to his next destination.

Calico Ghost Town.

Simon Cadabra kept the needle pegged at 80mph, swinging the Econoline van in and out through the light late night traffic and hoping that the relatively boring appearance of the standard Ford van would prevent him from getting a ticket. He knew that the CHP more often pulled over sports cars and sportier SUVs, almost always the red ones, which is why Cadabra had chosen something as plain vanilla as a white Ford Econoline.

The girl, Anjelica, sat in the passenger seat beside him, staring stoically straight forward at the road ahead of them. Cadabra felt a little pang of guilt as he looked down at the silver duct tape he had wrapped around her shoulders and the back of the seat but he couldn't take any chances. She had escaped from him once, with the assistance of the private dick, of course, and that wasn't going to happen again.

"Mister, where are you taking me?" Anjelica asked. Cadabra frowned. Back at the waterpark, he had considered taping up her mouth as well as her shoulders. Instead, he decided to go with a verbal warning to save time. So far, in the nearly eight minutes since he'd pulled back onto the freeway, the girl hadn't taken his warning seriously, asking him approximately every forty-five seconds about where they were going.

Besides, she knew where they were going as well as he did. She had to.

"I told you to be quiet," Cadabra said. Again.

"But it stinks in here," Anjelica said. "I want to get out!"

Cadabra couldn't disagree with her about that. The van absolutely reeked of demons, demons that, as far as Cadabra knew, were all dead now. The stench of their leathery red skin and stale dead breath permeated the van, and Cadabra was glad it was just a rental. *Let* Hertz *deal with the stink,* Cadabra thought. *Their van, their problem.*

The headlights caught a standard green highway sign that read "Calico Ghost Town, Next Right." But Cadabra's triumphant grin transformed into a grimace of frustration as he read the next line: "Open daily 9:00am – 5:00pm except Christmas Day." *Open 9 to 5?* he thought. *Was this a town or another goddamn amusement park?*

He eased the van off Insterstate-15 and took the off-ramp with his foot on the brakes, slowing the van to a stop when he hit Calico Road and then taking a hard right. He followed Calico road for about five minutes in nearly complete darkness and then took another right at Ghost Town Road where a ten foot tall plywood miner stood holding a spade and a sign that read "Calico Ghost Town."

Cadabra followed Ghost Town Road for about half a mile, flicking on the van's brights so he could see farther head of him. The two lane, one-way road was rough and ancient, and was lined with antique fire engines, abandoned mining cars and broken wagon wheels.

A small wooden shack emerged out of the darkness and Cadabra's earlier question was answered. Calico Ghost Town wasn't really a town and it wasn't an amusement park. According to the sign attached to the front of the wooden shack, it was one of San Bernardino's Regional Parks. Now he understood the "Open Daily" sign he'd seen earlier. Fortunately, the shack was unmanned at this hour and there was no crossbar blocking entry so Cadabra drove on. He passed the empty parking lot and more antique mining equipment and arrived at a sign that hung over the roadway.

CALICO GHOST TOWN.

Largest Silver Mining Camp in California.

1881-1896

Below the welcome sign was another wooden sign, black with bright yellow letters carved into it. Cadabra pulled the van close and read:

Calico is an old West mining town that has been around since 1881, during the largest silver strike in California. With its 500 mines, Calico produced over $20 million in silver ore over a 12-year span. When silver lost its value in the mid-1890s, Calico lost its population. The miners packed up, loaded their mules, and moved away, abandoning the town that once gave them a good living. It became a ghost town.

Walter Knott purchased Calico in the 1950s, architecturally restoring all but the five original buildings to look at they did in the 1880s ...

Blah, blah, blah, Cadabra thought. He turned to Anjelica and asked, "So. You ever been to a ghost town?"

And he laughed at her wide-eyed reply of "Ghost?" *Scared of ghosts. Good. That means she'll stay close.*

He drove through yet another, smaller parking lot and entered the town. *They could shoot a spaghetti western here,* Cadabra thought. Although the road was roughly paved, the buildings were all made of wood, even the second story balconies and their rickety-looking railings. Signs in Old West fonts read CALICO HOUSE RESTAURANT, CALICO CANDLE COMPANY, ASSAYING and THE WAY IT WAS (which Cadabra assumed was a museum of some sort). In the distance, at just the point where the headlights reached their farthest, Cadabra saw a sign that read CALICO CEMETARY.

Although the place seemed empty, Cadabra kept his eyes open for any sign of a roving security guard or guard dog. Once, his heart jumped in his chest when he saw someone standing near the entrance of the GENERAL MERCHANDISE STORE, but it wound up being only a life-sized wooden cowboy, his hand on the carved pistol in the holster at his side and a shiny black mustache taking up much of the space on his wooden face.

Cadabra stopped the van in front of a wooden shack boasting a sign that read MARSHAL'S OFFICE and laughed smugly at the empty wooden coffin displayed out front. "This is as good as anywhere," he said to Anjelica. There was a snick and a switchblade suddenly appeared in his hand, its vengeful blade shining in what little light there was. He cut away the duct tape from Anjelica's seat and reached past her, pushing open her door.

"Okay," he said. "Let's go see what you're made of."

He cracked open the door, climbed out of the van, closed the door behind him and walked around the front to the passenger side.

Of course, the girl was gone.

Cadabra's hands balled into fists and he cursed himself for being so stupid.

Richard Keane had been lucky. He'd kept the Charger's speedometer pegged between 95 and 100 all the way from Lake Dolores and had managed to arrive at the Calico Ghost Town off-ramp unimpeded. Mary Shelley had warned him that Interstate 15 was crawling with CHP but he hadn't seen one in the ten minutes since he'd left the waterpark. Now, he was off the freeway and on Calico Road, following the street signs to Calico Ghost Town.

He only hoped he wasn't too late.

Keane turned right at the giant plywood miner and zipped by the guard shack as if it didn't exist. As he passed the lower parking lot, he punched the switch and the headlights blinked off. Keane slowed and drove in silence and darkness, the window down, his ears straining to find any unusual sound over the Charger's growling engine.

There weren't many roads in the Ghost Town itself and it didn't take Keane long to come across the Econoline. He let the Charger coast to a halt about a hundred yards back and killed the engine, waiting and listening.

If there was anybody in the Econoline, it seemed they weren't aware of Keane's arrival. The doors remained closed and the lights remained off. There was no exhaust streaming from the rear pipe which meant the engine wasn't running.

He toyed with the idea of re-starting the Charger and flooring it, thinking if he rammed the Econoline hard enough he could disable it. But he didn't know where Anjelica was and he couldn't risk injuring her. So, instead, he flipped the dome light switch from "Door" to "Off," gently opened the driver side door and stepped out.

He crept quietly toward the van, Whisper at the ready, damning each step as it crunched in the gravel as he neared. He knew that someone in the driver's seat of the van could easily see him approaching in the side view mirror so he crept up as far as he dared. At the last second, he leaped forward, shoving the gun through the open driver's side window, ready to pull the trigger.

The van was empty.

Keane slumped. *Where the hell were they?* Had Cadabra taken Anjelica somewhere to observe her, to try and get her to show him what her purpose here was? Or had something worse happened and Cadabra was out there somewhere trying to hide a body.

A cold chill settled over Keane that was followed almost instantly by an angry heat. *If he's hurt her,* Keane thought, *then Hell will be the least of his worries.*

To his right, on the road ahead of him, Keane heard a muffled voice. He couldn't make out the words, but it was a voice, all right, and deep enough to be Cadabra's. He crept back to the edge of the road and inched forward, his pant leg brushing the edge of the boardwalk lining the storefronts. The gravel still crunched underfoot, but Keane was convinced that staying on the gravel was quieter than on the squeaky wooden planks that made up the boardwalk.

He heard the voice again, a deep male voice apparently attempting to be soothing, and this time he heard the words.

"Come on, Anjelica," Simon Cadabra cooed. "Come on out, sweetie. Uncle Simon's gonna find you anyway."

So, she got away from him, Keane thought, *Good for her*. He stepped gingerly forward, his eyes searching. There, in the darkness about thirty feet in front of him, he could barely make out a shape, a paler gray blackness set against a sea of Stygian dark. Then the shape solidified as it stepped deeper into the dusty street. There was no mistaking Cadabra, all six foot seven of him, his back to Keane. Keane held his breath and watched as the big man stalked the storefronts and horse rails, pulling back canvas tarps and peering into dark corners.

Looking for the girl.

Whisper came up to bear. Keane took careful aim at the back of Cadabra's massive head, and his finger tightened on the trigger.

And then someone burst out of a doorway just a few feet in front of Cadabra and raced up the street ahead of him. *Anjelica!* Cadabra roared like an angry lion and charged after her. Keane pulled the trigger on his .45 but the hesitation cost him. His shot missed its mark, sending wood splinters flying, and Cadabra dropped to the ground and whirled, returning fire with a blast from his mammoth shotgun. Pinball-sized buckshot tore up the pavement beside Keane's feet. He fell back against the wooden wall, breathing heavily and trying to clear his ears of the thunderous firearm blasts.

Keane pressed flat against the wall, his ears straining for any sound through the cotton-ball static that was the result of the explosive roars. There was a sound of a rusty gate opening and Keane took a chance peek, seeing Anjelica at the end of the street, pulling open the black wrought iron gates to the Calico Cemetery and disappearing inside.

Another shotgun blast chased Keane back against the wall. More wooden slivers flew through the air, some burying themselves in his cheek and forehead.

"Ya see that?! She's in the graveyard, Dick!" Cadabra taunted. "That's our territory! The dead are ours!"

"Don't call me Dick!" Keane shouted back, jumping sideways across the wooden pathway and firing Whisper as fast as he could pull the trigger.

But he was too late. Keane's slugs bit into wooden walls hungrily but missed their target completely. Cadabra had already moved from his pinned-down safe place and was halfway through the cemetery gates, his triumphant grin visible even from this distance. Keane cursed and dashed for the cemetery.

The gate creaked loudly as Keane pushed through it but there was no anticipated shotgun fire. He stepped to the side of the gate and fell against the stone wall, listening. It was quiet. Either Cadabra had continued after Anjelica or he had fallen in an empty grave and broken his neck. Keane liked the second option much better but knew he wouldn't be that lucky. He edged into the cemetery grounds and his eyes began to adjust to the even thicker darkness here.

There weren't a lot of places to hide, Keane thought, as the scene before him faded into view. The cemetery was little more than row after row of raised dirt mounds, each about the size of a human body, with only the occasional grave marker and/or tumble weed commemorating the dead. There was no sign of the girl and no sign of Cadabra, just grave after grave after grave after grave. Fifty or more, Keane guessed, but he by no means had time for an exact count.

And then a gun barrel the size of an exhaust pipe was pressed behind his left ear. "Put down that archaic weapon," said Cadabra. "Or I'll blow your head clean off."

Dirty Harry, thought Keane. *1971. Clint Eastwood. Don Siegel.*

What would Clint do?

Keane opened his hand and let Whisper drop to the dirt. If he didn't, he'd die right here, right now. By doing what Cadabra had asked, at least he'd bought a couple of seconds.

"I could kill you right now," Cadabra said, as if reading Keane's thoughts. "But there's something I want you to see first." He nudged Keane with the barrel of the shotgun. "On your knees," he ordered.

Keane dropped to a kneeling position and Cadabra stepped closer behind him, the shotgun still pressed tightly against Keane's ear. They stared out at the empty cemetery and Keane wondered what the dead magician had up his sleeve, perhaps literally. He waited, his mind racing for a solution, a way out of this. A way to get to Anjelica.

"Ready?" Cadabra asked. "Watch this." He took a deep breath and then bellowed a series of phrases that Keane guessed were either Satanic chants or really bad Italian.

Nothing happened.

"That was great," Keane said. "You might want to see about getting a refund on your Rosetta Stone."

"Wait," said Cadabra ominously.

And then Keane saw it. A grave near the end of the third row on the left began to smoke as though something beneath it was smoldering. A moment later, another nearby grave began to do the same. Then a third. A fourth. A fifth.

As Keane watched with rising concern, he realized that the graves weren't *smoking*, they were belching up dust. *Something underneath was trying to get out.*

The dead are ours, Cadabra had said.

And there were a dozen of them now.

A few of the graves had stopped smoldering and something else was happening. Thin, transparent sheets began rising up out of the graves, billowing like cheesecloth in the wind. It almost looked as though someone was pulling a Kleenex out of the slot on top of the box. They waved and rippled and floated over the graves and, after a few unsure moments, they began to take form.

Keane began to recognize diaphanous human forms. Now standing on the first grave was a gold miner, complete with helmet, holding his pickax proudly over his shoulder. Before him was another, a lumberman, two deadly axes crossed across his chest. A third gauzy man appeared, this one apparently a blacksmith, the edges of the mighty farrier hammer in his hands glowing with an infernal orange fire.

A murmuring drone began to crawl across the cemetery and Keane winced as it grew into a low, guttural moan. The dead didn't want to be disturbed, but this man had disturbed them. They were bound by his command. It was their duty to do his bidding.

But that didn't mean they had to be happy about it.

"Find the girl!" Cadabra ordered his long dead but newborn army. "Find her and bring her to me."

Keane tried to jerk himself free but Cadabra was ready for him. "What's the matter?" he asked. "Don't like the show?"

"Go to hell, you prick."

"That's the idea," Cadabra laughed.

There were perhaps twenty of them now, transparent, colorless, some of them still seeping from their grave, others floating solemnly through the graveyard, stalking Anjelica, desperate to please their master and to get back to their eternal slumber.

They didn't have to wait long.

Suddenly, at the opposite end of the cemetery, the glow of a flashlight lit up a corner grave, and Anjelica's silhouette rose from behind one of the few headstones.

"Oh," said Cadabra. "There you are."

"Get down, Anjelica!" Keane yelled, only to earn a thump on the back of his head courtesy of Cadabra's meaty fist.

The ghosts stopped in place and turned to face the girl. For a moment, the graveyard was swathed in complete and utter silence.

And then Anjelica opened her arms in a welcoming fashion (a *Christ*-like fashion, Keane thought) and, although it was pitch black except for the flashlight bathing her in a soft light, he swore he could see her beatific smile.

"What makes you think …" Anjelica called to Cadabra. "… that the dead are *all* yours?"

She raised her hands higher in a motion that made Keane think of a snow angel, or a successful football goal. *Or the "Y" in YMCA. Village People, 1978.*

And the remaining graves began to smoke and new figures were rising out of the mounds of dirt and rocks. They formed into more of the same: Miners. Blacksmiths. Lumbermen. But there were others here as well: A sheriff, his silver star shining in the moonlight for the first time in 80 years. A gunslinger, the six-shooters at his hips heavy in their holsters but anxious to be freed. A schoolteacher, armed with a paddle and a chalk eraser.

And this group didn't moan in pain and displeasure. Instead, their voices were low and quiet. They had been called to get a job done and their ghostly grim and determined faces were hard evidence that they intended to do exactly that.

Keane looked up into Cadabra's face and saw disbelief and something else there. Terror, perhaps. Clearly, this was not the outcome he had anticipated.

"What?" Cadabra said, his voice wavering. "No ..."

He took a step back and Keane saw his chance. He grabbed the huge open mouth of the shotgun and rammed it back into Cadabra. The stock crashed into Cadabra's chin and the big man stumbled and then fell, a plume of dust rising from the impact. Keane leapt for his own pistol, for Whisper, and his fingers had almost clawed around it when a giant boot crashed down on them, crushing them, breaking them, snapping muscle and bone like hard candies. He cried out and looked up to see Cadabra's angry face.

"No," Cadabra said, grabbing Keane by the collar and lifting him to his feet. "It's not gonna be that easy."

He turned his attention to his ghostly minions. "Destroy them!" he cried, raising both fists in the air in triumph. "Kill them all!" He paused. "And then kill the girl!"

The resentful moaning and the determined drone of the opposing dead forces crashed together and became a banshee scream as they rushed toward each other, ghostly axes falling, spectral guns blasting, dead fists rising and falling.

It was the strangest and by far the eeriest battle Keane had ever seen.

He saw an evil-grinned blacksmith crash his farrier hammer into the skull of a female school teacher, her ethereal head collapsing and spilling out transparent blood and gray cotton candy matter that floated away into the night sky. And then the blacksmith was run through by a transparent figure that looked a lot like General George Custer (although Keane was certain it couldn't be).

As the battle raged on, the dead began to fall again. Severed pieces of clothing and body parts littered the ground, screams of pain and grunts of battle filled the air.

Silver blood spattered across the graveyard as the violence grew to a fever pitch.

Even in the shimmering black-and-white imagery before him, the gruesome carnage horrified Keane. He had never seen two armies fight so viciously. There were no rules to this battle; it was win at any cost, at any cost whatsoever. As if to prove that point, a ghostly soldier reached out with his right hand, dug his thumb into the left eye socket of what looked like a former butcher, and then slammed a bayonet into the center of the butcher's bulbous nose. That action was answered by an ethereal cowboy, who draped a dead man's noose over the soldier's head, tossed the line over the CALICO CEMETARY sign, and lifted the soldier into the air, where he twitched and clutched at his throat until he went still.

Soon, it became clear that Anjelica's side was winning.

Keane chanced another glance up at Cadabra who wore a stark, disbelieving look. The man appeared beaten, both strategically and physically, and perhaps broken as well. His best-laid plans had imploded beneath him and, as his last ghostly soldier expired beneath the black-gloved hands of one of Angelica's many still-standing spirits, Keane saw the moment he was looking for.

He dropped to his knees again, snatched up Whisper with his good hand, and turned the weapon up toward Cadabra's head.

Cadabra didn't even realize what was happening until just before the hammer fell. "No," he said weakly. "Please …"

Keane shot him twice in the jaw just beneath the chin and, again, the big man went down like a three hundred and twenty-five-pound bag of potatoes, a cartoonish cloud of dust rising around him.

Wincing at the throbbing pain from his ruined hand, Keane stuffed Whisper into his waist band and forced himself to his feet.

Most traces of the defeated ghosts were gone. Their severed limbs, their tattered clothing and their discarded weapons had vanished. Their graves were quiet once again. The victors were returning slowly to their eternal slumber, hovering above their individual mounds and then fading into the dirt, their duty completed.

Keane looked across to the opposite side of the graveyard to see Anjelica lower her arms as the flashlight nearby her winked out. A moment later, she appeared almost magically by his side. She took his ruined hand and he was astonished to realize that it felt all right now. The pain was gone.

"Where's your flashlight?" he asked her, seeing that her hands were empty.

"What flashlight?" Anjelica said.

"Never mind," Keane said. "Are we done here?"

Anjelica nodded.

"Then I guess it's on to Vasquez Rocks," Keane said, leading Anjelica back to the Charger.

CHAPTER TWENTY

The first words to reach Simon Cadabra's groggy, re-awakening mind were "Really? You're back again?" It was the disgusted voice of his supervisor, the skeleton-like Clay Watkins, and Cadabra's heart sank as he realized he was back in Watkins' dull gray office, the artificial lighting there sucking out what was left of his soul.

"He had more help this time," Cadabra said once he caught his breath. "They outnumbered and overpowered us."

"They?"

"Yes, they," Cadabra snapped. "Next time warn me that their side has an army of the dead, too. That would have been information I could have used."

"It's in the handbook," Watkins said flippantly, waving his hand in the air in dismissal. "But you've got bigger worries. The Boss is watching this one. Directly involved, they tell me. I got an e-mail from my supervisor this morning that says The Boss isn't happy with the way this is going and he's thinking about replacing you."

"In my dreams," Cadabra said. He scratched the new scar material beneath his chin, not liking the way the smooth flesh there puffed out. He wished there were a mirror in Watkins' gray office, so he could see if the damage was visible or if he could hide it with a collar or something.

Maybe an ascot.

"I don't think you understand me," Watkins said, his tone somber. "*He's* thinking about replacing you. Not, he's thinking of someone else to replace you, but he, himself, is thinking about replacing you."

"The Boss wants to take over?" Cadabra said dubiously. "Personally?"

"That's what I hear," Watkins said. "This mission is important to him and you haven't exactly given a stellar performance. As I told you in your last performance review, you need to buck up. You tend to take your missions too lightly, don't put your back into them. That's why you fail so often."

"I've never failed a single mission!" Cadabra spat. "You've never told me to 'buck up.'"

"That's not the point," Watkins said. "The point is that, now, you've got to buck up."

Cadabra shook his head in frustration. "So, am I going back or not?"

"The Boss decided to give you one more chance," Watkins said. "Against my recommendation, I might add."

"Thanks for your support."

"So, yes, you're going back. One last time. And I mean *one last time*," Watkins said. "Screw this up and you're done. Back to the cheating husband circuit."

Cadabra thought that, at this point, the cheating husband circuit didn't sound so bad.

"Don't look so depressed," Watkins said. "This time we've got a plan in place. It was obvious you needed some help, so we've given you some."

"A plan?"

"Oh, yes," Watkins said. "This private dick, what's his name … Keane?"

Cadabra nodded his head.

"He's spent a long time Betwixt, keeping up with what's going on in the world by watching lots of television: News, movies, TV shows, etc. Plus, he had internet access." Watkins held his palm to his mouth and whispered conspiratorially, "Better speeds than we've got, from what I've been told."

Cadabra nodded as though he were interested but couldn't have been less so.

Watkins dropped his hand. "We don't know much about him, but we know this: All those years of watching television have turned him into a geek. He loves movies and he loves television shows."

"So, what are you going to do?" Cadabra asked dryly. "Cut his cable?"

Watkins stared at him with venom, which was pretty effective, Cadabra thought, considering how much the guy looked like a snake. An old, withered, starving snake.

"No," Watkins said. "We're going to use that against him."

"How?"

Watkins reached into one of his desk drawers and produced a screw-cap Mason jar, filled with a thick yellow liquid.

Floating in the liquid was a wrinkled gray mass, about the size of a fist.

"What the hell is that?" Cadabra asked with revulsion.

"It's a demon brain," Watkins said. "From one of your team. They weren't of much use to you back at Lake Dolores, but this one's going to be very useful to us here." He held the jar up in front of his eyes, the distorted image of his face through the glass making Cadabra even queasier. "You know, of course, that demons thrive on the fears of their victims," Watkins asked.

"Yes," Cadabra responded. Of course, he did. That was in the handbook, too.

"They do this by absorbing the fears of their victim when they are in proximity. This particular demon got very close to your friend Richard Keane. Close enough to bite his face off."

"Almost," Cadabra amended.

"Yes," Watkins acquiesced. "Almost. But quite close enough to capture these ..."

He set the Mason jar on the desktop and his bony fingers unscrewed the lid. Almost immediately, the demon brain began to glow a pulsating orange red, as though a fire had ignited inside. As Cadabra watched, tiny black dots began to form around the edges of the brain. A moment later, they seemed to ignite beneath the liquid surface and float to the top where they lifted into the air, hovering between Cadabra and Watkins like fiery gnats or slow-motion fireworks.

"What *is* that?" Cadabra asked. He leaned in, taking a closer look, and swore he could see moving images inside the little dots, like miniature movies captured on tiny screens of smoke.

"Those are Mr. Keane's fears," Watkins said, with a smug smile. "Pick a couple. We'll put them to work."

Cadabra leaned forward even more, putting his face closer to the sputtering red dots, and smiled.

"You know," he said. "This just might work."

Private Investigator Richard Keane glanced down at the little girl who was the basis of his latest case and felt a sad smile on his face. Anjelica was sound asleep in the passenger seat beside him and her name had never been more descriptive.

She had fallen asleep about fifteen minutes south of Calico, asking only "Where's Reverend Mother?" to which Keane had grimly replied that he didn't know. Anjelica accepted the news somberly and had faded off to sleep shortly after.

Keane hoped her dreams were sweet but knew they would not be. She'd been through a lot. More than any little girl ever should be.

They were about an hour away from Aqua Dulce, where Vasquez Rocks was located, and Keane was looking forward to the visit. It was a place he was quite familiar with although he'd never physically been there.

He knew from Wikipedia that Vasquez Rocks was formed by rapid erosion and "uplift" (something that Keane had looked up at the time but had subsequently forgotten what it was) about twenty five million years ago and was later exposed by activity along the San Andreas Fault. He knew that the rocks got their name from outlaw Tiburcio Vasquez who had hidden out there between 1873 and 1874.

But the main reason that Vasquez Rocks was so familiar to him was because they were so often featured in movies and television. Keane had seen the area featured in *Werewolf of London*, vintage Westerns like *Bonanza* and *Apache*, the classic sci-fi shows *Outer Limits* and *Star Trek*, and even in ridiculous comedies like *Bill & Ted's Bogus Journey* and TV's *The Big Bang Theory*. The unique rock formations were perfect for communicating strange, new worlds and had been used in hundreds of feature films, television series, music videos and even a video game (that Keane had only read about).

So, like a tourist, Keane was looking forward to seeing Vasquez Rocks in the flesh. He hoped that it would be a quick visit without incident, but he knew that Simon Ca-dabra would probably be there waiting. *Like a bad penny*, Keane thought, *that guy just keeps turning up.*

Keane took the ramp off the Interstate 15 at Victorville and turned right onto Highway 18. He knew to follow the Pearblossom Highway through to Highway 14 which would take him to Vasquez Rocks in about twenty minutes, so they were a little over an hour away. Good. An hour of sleep would be good for Anjelica and it would give him time to think.

He drove by a McDonald's advertising DRIVE-IN OPEN 24 HOURS and, although he would have loved to stop there for one of those Egg McMuffins or McGriddle sandwiches he'd heard so much about, he didn't want to awaken Anjelica. *No,* he thought, i*t'll be better to drive straight through.*

And so he did.

It was Quarterback Donny Bennett's first Superbowl, and he had never felt better in his entire life.

He took his place behind center Carlton Parker, hands cupped, and barked out a few numbers. A split second later, the ball was snapped and Bennett snatched it away, stepped back and looked for his receiver, Quentin Dunlap, who was supposed to be halfway to the goal by now.

But Quentin was covered, and Bennett's blockers were getting mowed down.

Bennett scanned the field. There was *nobody* open. He lifted the ball as if to pass it and then brought it back down. *Nobody open at all.*

Out of the corner of his eye, he saw one of his team members go down, and then there was a mountain of a man charging at him, his mouth twisted in an insane grimace of triumph. Bennett lifted the ball again, trying to find somewhere to throw it, anywhere ...

And then one of Bennett's blockers was there, crashing helmet first into the opposing player's chest, knocking him down and around Bennett, clearing the quarterback's path.

And Bennett looked forward and saw an open pathway that led all the way to the goal line.

Bennett wasn't well known for his running game. He was a passer, first and foremost, and only ran when there was no other option. This was different somehow. It seemed to be not just the only way to go but the best way to go.

It seemed like destiny.

Bennett tucked the ball tightly against his body and started running. He felt as though the open space between him and the goal line was lit from above, as though some divine being was guiding him to his first Superbowl victory.

As he ran, he was only slightly aware of opposing players nearing him and then being knocked away by his team. Then he felt himself pulling ahead as the others lost speed or gave up. The goal line grew larger and larger as it got closer and closer and then Bennett could hear the bell! The bell was ringing! And ringing and ringing, and it wouldn't stop ringing.

Donny Bennett opened his eyes and found himself staring up at the ceiling in darkness. He was at home, in bed, in the middle of the night. His wife, Doris, lay beside him.

It had all been a dream. Even though he had been one of the most respected quarterbacks in NFL history in the late 90s, he had never made it to the big game. That dream had been the closest he had ever come to it.

"You gonna answer that or what?" Doris said in that sleep-thick voice that wives only ever let their husbands hear.

The phone, Donny thought. *The phone is ringing.*

He rolled onto his side and grabbed his reading glasses, sliding them onto his ears and settling them on the bridge on his nose a little awkwardly. He glanced first at the clock on the dresser and then at the iPhone flashing beside it. *One twenty?* Donny thought, perturbed. *Who the hell calls at 1:20?*

He plucked the iPhone from the dresser top and glanced at its bright display. "Winston Calvert," the iPhone proudly displayed. "New York."

"It's Winston," Donny said to Doris, who didn't hear him because she was already fast asleep again.

"Good morning, Winston," Donny said after accepting the call. "Is there a particular reason you're calling me at one in the morning?"

"You think that's bad," Calvert said. "It's four o'clock here."

"That's right," Donny replied. "So, what gives?"

"Well, I didn't think you'd want to wait to hear this news."

"What news?"

"It's about Lake Dolores."

Donny sat up straighter in bed. "What about it?"

"The Japanese are in," Calvert told him. "They'll supply the necessary funds to complete our purchase and to fund the first year's operation."

"You're shitting me."

"I would not shit you," Calvert said, laughing. "You're my favorite turd."

"But why now?"

"I don't know," Calvert said. "I thought the deal was dead in the water. I mean, I thought we had them when we pitched it six months ago. Who wouldn't want to fund a camp for disadvantaged youths run by the world's great living quarterback?"

"Greatest living *retired* quarterback," Bennett said.

"Greatest *ever*," Calvert added. "But when they didn't get back to me, despite numerous attempts, I figured they were just out. Then, this morning, out of the blue, I get an e-mail from their guy not only confirming they were in, but with a signed copy of the initial agreement attached."

"I just can't believe it," Bennett said. "Doris and I just figured it was over."

"Like I said, so did I," Calvert laughed again. "But I'm telling you, Donny. We're in business. You're going to give those kids the help they need."

"The help they *deserve*," Donny corrected.

"Yes," Calvert said. "Okay, Donny. I just wanted you to know as soon as I knew. Now go back to sleep."

Donny smiled. "I don't think I can," he said. "I don't think I'll sleep for the rest of the day."

"I'll give you a call later," Calvert said. "Go over the details."

"Thanks, Calvert."

"Thank *you*, Donny."

The iPhone signaled that the call had ended. Donny sat in stunned silence, the only sound in the room the antique clock on the far wall ticking down the seconds and the light whistle of Doris's breathing. Donny replaced the iPhone on the dresser and picked up a picture frame there.

It was a photo of Doris and their son, Andrew, taken at a charity event seven years ago. Although Andrew looked happy and healthy in the photo, Donny could see the shadows of demons in his eyes. The demons that would eventually kill him.

Andrew had died of a drug overdose shortly after that photo had been taken. As would any parent, Doris and Donny had taken it hard, but found some piece of solace in the creation of the Pro Football Players We Care Camp which they'd hoped to build both as a tribute to their lost son and as a beacon of hope for those youth who might have found themselves in the same situation.

It was a blatant cliché, but Donny truly believed that if they could save even one kid's life, it would all be worth it.

He put the photo back on the dresser and rolled over. He put his hand on Doris' shoulder and gently shook it.

"Doris, honey," he said. "Wake up. I've got some wonderful news."

The bright full moon bathed the sleeping town of Agua Dulce in a warm, bluish glow as Richard Keane eased the Charger onto the drive leading to Vasquez Rocks. Already, on their way in, he had recognized the shadows of rock formations that he had previously seen only on the TV in his office.

A sign reading VASQUEZ ROCKS COUNTY PARK (COUNTY OF LOS ANGELES; DEPARTMENT OF PARKS AND RECREATION) welcomed him.

Keane caught movement out of the corner of his eye and looked over to see Anjelica stirring. "Good morning, Princess," he said.

"I'm not a princess," Anjelica said without malice.

"Haven't you ever wanted to be a princess?" Keane asked. He thought all little girls wanted to be princesses.

"No," Anjelica said. "I haven't."

"Oh," Keane said. "Then what do you want to be?"

Anjelica looked up at him with her soulful, seven-year-old eyes. "Helpful," she said. "I want to be helpful."

"Helpful," Keane repeated. "I like that."

The park appeared to be deserted. *Probably*, Keane thought, *because it's the middle of the night and no one in their right mind would be out here in the dark.* He came to a locked gate and, with the tools he always kept on him, made quick work of the simple padlock hung there. He then guided the Charger into the park, stopped, and re-locked the gate behind him. He drove slowly through the empty parking area and brought the car to a halt near a trail entrance.

They sat for a moment in silence. Finally, Keane asked, "Okay. What now?"

Anjelica shrugged.

"Well, what say we go for a walk?" Keane suggested. "Maybe that will give us a hint. Nothing happens in fifteen minutes, I say we hit the road and continue on to Santa Barbara. Work for you?"

"Yes," Anjelica said.

They climbed out into the early morning air. It was slightly chilly, but not too bad, and Keane could tell that, when the sun came up in a few hours, it was going to be a nice clear day. He looked around in awe at the amazing rock formations that surrounded them. Layered rocks lay stacked on their sides, slanted at 45-degree angles, their pointed tips reaching for the sky. Everywhere he looked seemed to be familiar and, considering how many times Hollywood had used this area, he realized he probably had indeed seen it all before.

Keane found himself wishing it were later in the day so he could see the full glory of the area in sunlight. But today, he had business to tend to first.

Anjelica reached up and took his hand and the two of them walked onto the dirt pathway.

"Recognize any of these rocks?" Keane said.

"I don't," Anjelica said.

"They use them a lot in the movies and on TV," Keane told her.

"We don't have TV at the convent," Anjelica said.

"You don't?" Keane was surprised. "Oh, right," he added. "Probably didn't want it to rot your little mind."

"No," said Anjelica. "Cable was too expensive."

Keane nodded. "Makes sense," he said.

And they continued walking into the park.

Keane was struck by how much some of the formations looked alike. He thought he recognized a formation on the right as something he'd seen in *Star Trek*, but there was another formation on the left that looked nearly identical. Regardless, he was enjoying the quiet walk with Anjelica in the silvery moonlight.

He marveled at this little girl and what she'd been through in less than 24 hours. Virtually everyone she knew had been killed in that short span of time, violently, and yet she still soldiered bravely, faithfully, onward. She had seen things that no one, especially a not even eight-year-old girl, should ever see—machine-gun bearing nuns, teeth-gnashing demons, battling ghosts—and yet she hadn't even questioned her journey, much less given up on it.

Back at his office, when this thing first began, Keane remembered that Buster had told him how important this assignment was and now Keane could see why. This little girl was something special. He could sense that she was capable of greatness in her lifetime, and he was going to do his damnedest to make sure she made it to Santa Barbara, and to safety, under his watch.

As they walked, the only sound the crunching of their feet on the silty sand, Keane took in the magnificence around him. He had never been a religious man himself, wasn't even today despite the circumstances he now found himself in, but he wondered how could anybody *not* believe in a higher power while walking through a place of such complete majesty, beauty and serenity.

"Mr. Keane?" Anjelica asked in the silence. She kept her voice low, as if not to disturb the natural quiet of the early morning.

"Yes?"

"What will they do with me in Santa Barbara?"

"I don't know their plans," Keane said. "But I know they want to protect you."

"Protect me?" Anjelica asked. "From what?"

"I don't know that, either," he said. "But I know that they will. Will you miss Las Vegas?"

"I miss the people there."

"I know you do. And there's nothing I can say that will make that any easier." He stopped beneath a particularly striking rock formation and looked down at her.

"You'll love Santa Barbara, though," he said. "It's a beautiful town, full of history and sunshine. There are lovely museums there and I hear the zoo is great, too. I've always loved Santa Barbara. It's a town with a beating heart of its own. I used to vacation there a lot when I was … ("alive") …working."

"Do you miss where you come from?" Anjelica said.

Keane thought about that. He wasn't sure whether Anjelica meant did he miss Los Angeles or did he miss 1954. Or did he miss his little office floating around in space somewhere. "Yes," he finally answered. "And no. A little of both."

Anjelica looked up at him curiously. He gave her a comforting smile. "It's not so easy to decide when your life's been split up like mine has," he said.

"I understand," Anjelica said. And Keane was certain that she did.

A soft breeze whirled around them and Keane was surprised by its warmth in the darkness. They stood still a moment, enjoying the breeze and the brightness of the moon, and then continued onward.

Keane stopped suddenly. Anjelica walked a step ahead and he gently pulled her back by the hands they still held. She looked up at him sharply. He put a finger to his lips and then touched his ear.

The only sounds were those of the desert insects and of the freeway humming away in the distance. Keane concentrated. He was sure he'd heard something else. A moment passed and then, there it was again.

It was the same *crunch crunch* that his and Anjelica's feet had been making as they moved along the pathway. And it was coming from somewhere not too far behind them. He turned and looked back along the path, but it was empty for about 100 yards and then disappeared around a corner. He tilted his head, putting all his concentration into listening. Yes. There it was. Somebody was definitely coming.

Somebody a little slower than they were, he decided, based on their pace and somebody much heavier, based on the loudness of the crunching.

Cadabra, Keane decided. He was neither surprised nor disturbed. They had beaten the man at his own game so far and Keane was confident this outing would be no different.

He gently pushed Anjelica behind a large rock at the side of the path, putting his finger to his lips so she would remain silent. Then, he used hand signals to tell her to stay where she was while he went and stood in the middle of the path, Whisper hanging at his side. *No hiding this time,* Keane thought. *When he comes around that corner, I want him to see me and I want him to know that I am ready for him.*

The heavy crunching grew louder and Keane could tell that Cadabra was nearing the corner. Any second now, he'd come around the bend and Keane lifted his weapon to the firing position, ready for action. The sound of steps in gravel grew still louder and then someone came around the corner and stood there, staring down the open pathway at him.

But it wasn't Cadabra, Keane realized, and felt his blood run a little cold. It wasn't even human.

The thing at the other end of the pathway stood about six and a half feet tall. Its broad shoulders were massive and its arms and legs were cabled with hard muscle. It wore a shimmering gold tunic, spotted with red and brown circles, and it reminded Keane a little of a Roman citizen's toga.

Its skin was olive green. Its unreadable eyes were like clusters of diamonds compacted into twin orbs the size of a baseball. And its head was that of a giant lizard or crocodile, with a deep, savage mouth to match, lined with two-inch dagger-like teeth.

Keane recognized the creature from his years of television viewing. It was the Gorn, the villain from an old episode of *Star Trek* entitled "Arena." Keane knew it was 400 pounds of ferocious fighting muscle.

Suddenly, Whisper felt tiny in his hand and he wished he had spent less time watching TV for all those years in his Betwixt office. He was certain that the Gorn had been lifted from his own mind—where the hell else could it have come from?—and he cursed himself for allowing it to cross his memory.

At least I didn't think of the Zanti Misfits, Keane thought.

At the opposite end of the path, the Gorn growled deep in its throat, a sound somewhere between the low rumble of a tractor-trailer and the senseless mumbling of an angry homeless person. It unleashed a massive sword hung by a belt on its side.

And it charged.

Keane pulled the trigger on Whisper and the .45 bucked once, twice. The slugs hit the Gorn square in the chest and, although Keane couldn't be sure, it seemed to him that the bullets merely ricocheted off into the morning air, their impact not even slowing the oncoming attacker.

What did Captain Kirk do? Keane thought quickly. He remembered that, in the *Star Trek* episode, Kirk had built a firearm out of what looked like an old bamboo trunk, a handful of uncut diamonds and some handmade gunpowder. Compared to Keane's .45, however, Kirk's weapon had looked like a bazooka.

No time to build a bazooka, Keane thought. He braced himself as the ground vibrated beneath his feet with increasing intensity as the creature grew closer.

"Anjelica," Keane said aloud, without looking in her direction and giving away her position. "Stay down!" He braced himself, keeping his eyes on the Gorn's sword. The impact was going to be bad enough; he didn't need to be impaled at the same time.

This is going to be bad, Keane thought.

It was.

The Gorn hit him with all the power of a charging rhinoceros and Keane was just able to deflect the glittering sword it held and prevent himself from being speared alive. He felt what he was sure were ribs cracking as he was thrown up off the trail and into the rocks behind him, pistol and fedora flying, pain exploding in every inch of his body. He gasped for air, the wind knocked clean out of him, as he tried to scramble up to fend off the attack that was coming next. The Gorn, supposedly a slow creature according to *Star Trek*, found a burst of speed in its attack and was on him instantly, one of its mighty fists punching into him, its teeth slashing, its massive arm attempting to work the sword in at the right angle, to get its edge between his ribs or its point into Keane's soft belly.

Keane knew the sword would be the end of him and put everything he had into keeping it away. The rain of punches from the Gorn's free hand took their toll, but he kept his hands and feet at the sword, preventing its slashing edges and brutal cutting point from hitting their mark.

Somehow, Keane got his feet in the Gorn's midriff and heaved, pushing it away. It fell flat on its back on the pathway, raising a huge cloud of silty dust. Keane, trying to catch his breath, climbed unsteadily to his feet, and reached instinctively into his holster for Whisper, his eyes widening in dismay when he found the holster empty.

And then the Gorn swung out with its right leg and whipped Keane's legs out from underneath him. He went down with a heavy thump that shook him to his very core, and he swore he could hear more cracking of bone and tearing of ligaments as he fell back onto the rocks, his leg twisted beneath him at a seemingly impossible angle.

The Gorn rose above him, snickering in an ungodly wheeze. It scanned the ground around them, stepped away and quickly returned, carrying a huge boulder that Keane guessed weighed about as much as he did. Powerful muscles rippled beneath its scaly green skin as the reptilian monster raised the boulder up over its head and looked down at Keane with a triumphant glare.

Keane tried weakly to crawl away on his battered bones. He could only hold up a shaky hand, lamely trying to fend off what he knew was coming next, what he knew was inevitable.

The Gorn raised the rock higher and Keane heard it make one more wheezing grunt before it started to smash down ...

... And then there was another sound ...

... a *loud, roaring* sound ...

... And something smashed into the Gorn, sending it crashing to the ground, knocking the boulder out of its hands where it rolled away down the pathway harmlessly. A huge cloud of dust filled the air and, for a moment, Keane could see nothing.

As the dust faded away, Keane sat up painfully and shook his head in disbelief as he saw a woman straddling a Harley-Davidson Sportster, a submachine gun slung over her shoulder, a leather jacket one size too big for her draped over what Keane now realized was a nun's habit.

A nun's habit?

"Now that's what I call good timing, gumshoe," said Reverend Mother Mary Shelley, unslinging the MAC-11 from beneath her scapular and pointing its muzzle down into the Gorn's face. "Two seconds later and you would have been dead meat."

And she pulled the trigger and the Gorn's head exploded in a shower of green flesh, gray matter, and bright red blood.

Despite the pain furrowing through every inch of his body, Keane felt a happy smile form on his face. "How ...?" he began.

"No questions now," Mary Shelley said. "Where's my little girl?"

"What ...?"

"Where's Anjelica?"

Keane pointed weakly to the rock he'd hidden her behind. "She's over …" he said, and choked.

Because there was no one behind the rock any longer.

Anjelica was gone.

Reverend Mother Mary Shelley couldn't believe what Keane was telling her. She followed the private eye's pointing finger to a rock on the side of the road but she didn't see Anjelica.

"Over where, Mr. Keane?" Mary Shelley said.

"I told her to stay put," Keane told her. "I told her to stay down behind this rock."

He limped over and peeked behind the rock. Mary Shelley could see even from her position on the motorcycle that there was no way anyone was hiding there.

"Did she just wander away? Or did somebody take her?" she asked.

"I don't know," Keane replied. "I didn't see …"

"What do you mean, you 'didn't see?'" Mary Shelley barked. "You were supposed to be watching her, guarding her. She's the sole purpose of your assignment!"

"Well, you'll have to excuse me, lady," Keane said. "But I was getting my ass kicked by a giant lizard armed with a samurai sword!"

He was right, Mary Shelley realized. It was unfair for her to blame him for the girl's disappearance when a 400-pound warrior reptile figured into the mix. "I'm sorry," she said. "I'm just worried."

"Me, too," Keane said, approaching the motorcycle. "Scootch back and let's go find her."

"I beg your pardon?" asked Mary Shelley.

"Scootch back," Keane said again. "We'll take the bike and search the path ahead for her. She can't be far."

Mary Shelley shook her head. "No, *you* get on the back," she said. "It's 2015, Mr. Keane, not 1954. Times have changed. More importantly, this is *my* motorcycle. *You* get on the back, and we'll go look for her together."

Keane looked more than a little hurt. "Okay, okay," he said. "Don't get your panties in a bunch."

She gave him a glare that could have withered a desert cactus.

"Sorry, sister," he said, swinging his leg over the saddle and placing his feet on the back pegs

They rode along the dirt pathway slowly, peering into canyons and calling the girl's name. There was no sign of her. No response. They drove on.

After about fifteen minutes, Keane pointed to something on the pathway ahead of them. Mary Shelley squinted, saw a shadowy ... *something* ... crawling along the ground, at just the edge of the headlight's reach.

"Is that a dog?" Keane asked from behind her.

She looked again. It was about the size of a small dog, say, a Boston Terrier. But it moved differently, strangely.

"Doesn't look like a dog," Mary Shelley said. "More like a possum, or something."

They drove closer. As they neared the animal, it seemed to sense them and, rather than disappearing into the darkness, it became agitated and began moving faster, crawling toward them purposefully.

The motorcycle coasted toward the thing until they were close enough to see it and Mary Shelley heard Keane gasp behind her.

The thing was indeed the size of a small dog, but that's where all similarities ended. It was obviously a gigantic insect, with six segmented legs, a two-part body and a large, ant-like head. It stared up at them with two huge, human-like eyes burning with a hatred that was almost palpable. It had a human nose and a human mouth, twisted in a grimace of anger and malice

"What *is* that?" Mary Shelley asked, her voice thick with disgust.

"That..." Keane told her. "...is a Zanti Misfit. You know. From *The Outer Limits*?"

Mary Shelley shook her head.

"You really should have invested in cable," Keane said. He winced as the mother superior drove over the insect, crushing it beneath the Harley's tires like ...

... well, like a bug.

Simon Cadabra could see the light at the end of the tunnel.

He didn't know where the private eye was and, frankly, he didn't care. Last he'd seen, the Gorn was beating the crap out of the man, and that was just fine with Cadabra. He had snatched the girl from her hiding place, as private dick battled overgrown reptile, and carried her away. Now, climbing one of the many familiar rock formations located at Vasquez Rocks, he tugged at the girl, cursing her for resisting. Seriously, what was the point? Surely, she knew by now that it was all over. Keane could in no way defeat the Gorn and, even if by some miracle he did, he could never get to the girl. The Misfits would see to that.

Cadabra glanced around at the vast insectoid army beneath him. There were thousands of them, their wild human eyes staring up from fist-sized ant heads, their jaws working in a kind of barely contained fury. He laughed. It was so insanely beautiful, there was nothing else he could really do but laugh.

Cadabra was nearly to the top. He held Anjelica tightly by the wrist, tugging her behind him and, even though she showed no signs of fear, she was not making it easy on him. She dug her feet into the soil and yanked back on Cadabra's arm, resisting any way she could.

Not that it mattered, Cadabra thought. He reached the topmost part of the formation and stared down at the ground forty feet below him. It moved in the moonlight as though it were alive. *Because it is alive*, Cadabra thought, *alive with the Zanti Misfits that that poor TV-loving fool had unwittingly given them.*

Cadabra had to admit that, for once, Clay Watkins had been right. Using the demon brain to discover Keane's fears had led to the two images related to Vasquez Rocks that most affected him. There was the Gorn, whose brute strength and merciless philosophy made him seem frighteningly invincible. And there were the Zanti Misfits, a marauding infestation of dog-sized insects with sour human faces and deadly biting mouths, whose sole goal seemed to be the destruction of humankind.

No, Keane would not be riding up on his white horse and rescuing his beloved Anjelica this time. Unless he defeated the Gorn. Which was impossible, of course, because Keane was a maybe 200-pound human private eye, while the Gorn was a 400-pound intergalactic killer. And, if by some chance Keane *did* best the Gorn (and Cadabra had long since stopped underestimating the man), he would have to get through the Zanti Misfits, all five thousand of them, with their biting human faces and their foot-long insect bodies, before he could get to Cadabra and Anjelica.

And, by the time he does that, Cadabra thought, *I'll have killed the girl anyway.*

He stood at the precipice for a moment, soaking in the crisp, white moonlight, and then he turned to the girl. She stared up at him with eyes that were absent of malice or hatred, but instead communicated a kind of questioning that made Cadabra tilt his head, then shake it. He steeled himself, and then pushed the exhaust pipe-sized barrel of the shotgun up against the girl's right cheek.

Instead of the cry of fear that he expected, Cadabra was shaken when the girl pressed her cheek harder against the wide mouth of the shotgun, looked into Cadabra's eyes, and said, "It's okay, Mister. I understand."

Cadabra blinked. "Wh … what?"

"I said it's okay," the girl continued. "I understand why you have to do this." She didn't so much smile as nod with empathy. She reached up with her right hand and pressed the shotgun barrel against her temple.

Cadabra's eyes narrowed. He thought of Watkins, of the man's insults and lies. He thought of The Boss, threatening to come and do the job on his own if Watkins couldn't get someone to do it right. He thought of The Office, its gray walls and sterile lights. He thought of the men and women he had led to cheat against their loving spouses, promising them fleshly delights that would have been impossible to attain otherwise.

And he thought of this little, seven year old girl, telling a giant of a man that it was okay to kill her, to put a shotgun to her head and blow it clean off her shoulders. That she understood it was what he had to do. That she forgave him for the atrocity he was about to perform.

Cadabra's shoulders sank and his chin fell to his chest. He dropped the shotgun, which clattered to the rocks beneath him and then rolled off the cliff and over the edge, crash-landing in the sea of Zanti Misfits below, their bearded faces and furious eyes looking up in angry, buzzing confusion.

"Well, shit," Cadabra said. "I guess I can't do it after all."

He looked down at the girl's face and found her staring up into his eyes, a beatific smile of understanding and gratitude beaming up at him, shining like a beacon in the moonlight. Cadabra knew what that smile meant. To the little girl, it was pure and genuine gratefulness. To Cadabra it was the end. He had failed The Boss yet again and there would be no returning this time.

It was back to cheating spouses for Simon Cadabra. Or perhaps worse. Teaching kids to play with matches maybe.

Cadabra stood to his full height and stepped back, gazing into the glow of the full moon. He hadn't been this depressed since the immolation illusion went awry in Las Vegas and yet, there was something freeing about it, too. A new start? Nah. He knew better than that. But at least he could always say he didn't kill a little girl just because he was following orders.

He sighed deeply, stepped back, and felt a loose rock roll awkwardly beneath his boot. He tried to regain his balance with his other foot, but the ground was loose there, too. Before he knew it, he was stumbling backwards toward the edge of the cliff, arms pinwheeling madly. As he lost his balance completely, a strange calm came over him and he tumbled over the edge falling, reverse swan-dive style, into the seething mass of Zanti Misfits below. He fell into them with a sickening crunch, crushing several dozen of them with his 325-pound body, and then they swarmed over him, their vicious jaws biting, their crazed eyes rolling over in their heads. And Cadabra's calmness leapt away, like a ghost leaving its living body, and he screamed and screamed as they tore him to pieces, screamed until there was nothing left to scream with.

Anjelica stood at the top of the formation, looking down at the carnage below her, her heart filling with great sadness. She watched the Zantis flow over the dark shape of Simon Cadabra until they enveloped him and he disappeared beneath them.

A few moments later, they were done with him, pulling away and exposing his bloody, flesh-peppered bones, which glowed a sad, cold blue in the moonlight.

And then they were coming for her.

Anjelica stepped back from the edge. She looked back the way she and Cadabra had come. The Zantis were creeping up the formation toward her, their antennae twitching, their jaws snapping, their violent intentions apparent. She ran to the opposite side of the cliff and looked down. It was a fifty-foot drop and, if that didn't kill her, the river of Zantis there would.

There was no place to run. There were no weapons—other than small useless rocks—with which to defend herself. There was nothing to do but stand there and wait, while the Zantis crept closer, their teeth gnashing, their crazy eyes winking and blinking in an insane fury. They were almost at the top now, surrounding her, no more than ten feet away, and Anjelica realized with a profound disappointment much beyond her years that she had come to the end of her journey.

And then she heard it: a thick rumbling roar like that of a locomotive. She looked down near the bottom of the formation and she saw the Harley climbing up toward her, black smoke pouring out of its exhaust, its two riders kicking away at the sea of Zantis below their tires.

And Anjelica recognized the rider in front. Reverend Mother Mary Shelley! And she saw the rider in the back was Mr. Keane. A smile flashed across her face and she kicked out at the Zanti that jumped out at her, teeth flashing, and sent it sailing over the edge of the cliff.

This wasn't the end after all!

A moment later, the big motorcycle rolled to a rough stop beside her and Mr. Keane reached down and lifted her into the air, setting her down on the seat between the two riders.

"Reverend Mother!" Anjelica cried with joy, throwing her arms around Mary Shelley and hugging her close.

"Hi, honey," Mary Shelley said.

"Hold on tight, Anjelica," Keane told her, stepping on the head of a Misfit and crushing it like a cigar. "This is gonna be a rough ride."

And then they were going back down the way they came, grinding through the sea of Misfits like a Coast Guard cutter through ice. Shelley guided the motorcycle with precision through the throngs of little monsters and Keane beat them back with his boots and the sword he'd taken from the Gorn.

In mere seconds, they were at the bottom of the formation and rumbling back to the Charger.

** ** **

Keane dismounted in the parking lot and allowed Anjelica a quiet moment with the Reverend Mother before depositing her in the car. He opened the driver's door and climbed in, turned the big engine over, and rolled down the window.

"You coming with?" he asked the nun on the bike.

"Right behind you," Reverend Mother Mary Shelley said.

"Can't wait to hear the story about how you got this bike," Keane smiled.

"Plenty of time to tell that story," Mary Shelley said. "When we get to where we're going."

Keane nodded and stepped on the gas, zipping past a flustered park ranger who was just opening the main gates, Mary Shelley on her Sportster right behind them.

Only one more stop to go.

Santa Barbara.

Richard Keane wanted nothing more than to drive straight from Vasquez Rocks to the Santa Barbara mission. With Mary Shelley on the Sportster behind them, they followed the 14 freeway past Newhall and took a right over a sweeping bridge, merging onto the 5 North.

But Keane was filthy, sore, and sported open cuts that seeped blood. As they passed through Valencia, he gave a hand signal to Mary Shelley and they pulled off the freeway and stopped at a Tommy's Original Burger in Valencia. *If you don't see the shack*, said the sign on the front of the building, *Take it Back!* Keane saw the miniature red shack bursting out of the roof of the restaurant so he knew he wouldn't have to take it back.

It felt good to get out of the car and to stretch his sore arms and legs and he was pleased when Anjelica announced she was hungry. *Good*, he thought, *she needs to eat something.* "Quick stop," Keane explained as Mary Shelley joined them. "I want to get cleaned up, bandage some of these cuts, and grab a quick bite. Then we have to get back on the road. I'm sure Cadabra ... or his replacement ... won't be far behind."

"Sounds good," Mary Shelley said. "I could eat."

Once inside, Keane headed to the bathroom while Mary Shelley and Anjelica went to the counter and ordered food: three breakfast sandwiches on muffins, no egg or chili on one (Anjelica's).

The food came at just about the same time that Keane exited the bathroom. He sat down heavily in the red metal chair and rested his elbows on the clean white table. "I am very tired," he announced.

"You look like you've had a hard week," Mary Shelley said.

"I have," Keane added. "I've had a hard week in just the past twenty-four hours."

They shared a smile as Mary Shelley passed out the food. Anjelica took a big bite of her sandwich and grinned happily.

"You like that, huh?" Keane said. "One of these days, you'll like the chili, too. It's really good."

"When I grow up," Anjelica said.

"When you grow up," Keane agreed.

He bit into his sandwich and chili and melted cheese slid out of his mouth and onto the paper towel in front of him.

Anjelica laughed.

"Damn, that is good," Keane said, enjoying Tommy's legendary thick brown chili and the pile of pickles balanced on the center of the sandwich. "That's one thing I missed. Good ol' fast food. Didn't get any of that ... you know, out there." He rolled his eyes toward the sky.

He washed down another, bigger bite with a swig of Diet Pepsi and then looked across the table at Mary Shelley. "Okay, sister," he said. "Spill."

The Reverend Mother looked across the table at him, her eyes open wide with mock ignorance.

"Don't give me that," Keane said, laughing. "You know what I'm talking about. Last time I saw you, you were being chased into the darkness by a big, butt-ugly demon.

Then you show up on a motorcycle, a *Harley Davidson* of all things, still kicking ass and taking names. What happened?"

Mary Shelley put down her sandwich, wiped the excess chili off with a paper towel, and rested her hands on the table. She sighed. "It's all kind of a blur," she said. "It happened so fast and so … naturally."

"Go on," Keane said.

And Mary Shelley told them her story.

Chapter Twenty-Seven

Reverend Mother Mary Shelley was having a hard time keeping a grip on reality. She was standing in an abandoned waterpark, holding a sub-machine gun, talking with a dead private eye and a giant magician/kidnapper who had burned himself to death on stage several years before.

She'd been warned and trained and prepared for years that this day was coming but, now … now that it was here … everything seemed so *surreal*.

"So, here's what we're going to do," said the magician/kidnapper, who had just introduced himself as Simon Cadabra. "I'm going to take dear Anjelica here with me so she and I can discuss what it is she's supposed to accomplish on this journey of yours. *Her mission*, I'm going to call it. In the meantime, allow me to introduce you to my little friends."

Who does this guy think he is? Mary Shelley thought. *Scarface?*

And then she wrinkled her nose at the sudden odor, a stench like that of wet dogs on fire, and something came charging out at them from the shadows. There were five of them and they looked like dogs at first, or wolves, but as they came closer she could see that their skin was red and their heads, almost human, sported pointed ears and two tiny horns. They bared needle teeth and they scraped the ground with razor sharp nails and it was obvious they were coming in for the kill.

They looked like demons from hell!

The sound of a nearby gunshot snapped her out of her disgusted horror and she saw Private Investigator Richard Keane lift his .45 and put a bullet in the face of closest demon. It cried out in agony and then curled up and died, just like a spider sprayed with Raid. Mary Shelley lifted her MAC-11 and fired a burst into the belly of the demon rushing for her. For a microsecond, she felt horror as the thing took the shots and yet kept coming!

"No!" she heard the private eye yell at her through the gunfire and the demonic screams. "The head! Shoot them in the head!"

Black blood spilled from the bullet wounds in the demon's belly as it leapt into the air, its jaw opening more than should have been possible as it reached hungrily toward her throat. Mary Shelly re-positioned the MAC-11 and put a burst of slugs through the roof of its mouth. The thing exploded in a cloud of rancid meat as though there had been a grenade in its throat. What was left of its shattered body fell wetly to the dusty ground there. The smell of cordite blended with the scent of rotting meat.

Mary Shelley saw another demon slam into Keane and knock him to the ground. She took aim, but couldn't risk a shot for fear she might hit the P.I., too. She caught another movement out of the corner of her eye and was horrified to see that the magician had taken the girl and gone.

And then there was the fifth demon, ten feet away, creeping stealthily toward her, its yellow eyes watching her gun hand closely.

Mary Shelley pointed the MAC-11 in the direction of the fifth demon and pulled the trigger. The weapon spat one single bullet and then froze.

Jammed.

She could almost see the demon's victorious smile.

There were two choices. Stand here and fight the demon hand to hand, in which battle she would no doubt be torn to shreds by its filthy nails and sabre teeth, or run into the desert night, try to find place to hide in the abandoned waterpark beyond, clear her weapon or get her hands on another that would give her at least a chance against defeating the demon.

Praying that Keane would be okay on his own, she ran blindly into the unbroken darkness behind her.

The demon, with an amused, hungry look on its hideous red face, chased after her.

** ** **

"I ran back into the waterpark," Mary Shelley told Keane and Anjelica. They had both forgotten their Tommy's breakfast sandwiches and were listening to her tale with rapt attention. "There were old waterslide tunnels everywhere. I ran until I was sure I'd lost the demon, and then I climbed inside one of those tunnels and waited."

** ** **

Mary Shelley knew that the waterslide tunnel she was hiding in had once been full of rushing water, but it was dry as a bone now, having sat in the hot, acrid desert air for several years, perhaps even a decade.

She tried furiously to clear her weapon, but it was jammed solid. She yanked at the bolt, set the safety to on, jerked out the magazine. Tapped it on the ground, hoping a bullet would fall out. Slammed the cartridge back home. Released the safety. Pulled the trigger.

Nothing.

She could hear the demon's heavy breathing in the otherwise still night air. It was closing in on her position. She yanked at the bolt and removed the magazine again.

She took a deep breath, tried to calm herself. Willed her training to come back to her.

Step 1: Lock back the bolt.

Step 2: Put weapon on SAFE.

Step 3: Check or replace magazine.

Replace magazine! She yanked out the old magazine, tossed it noisily to the tunnel floor, and reached inside her habit, digging at an inside pocket there. She pulled out a new magazine, slammed it home, released the bolt. It felt right ...

... but there was no time to test it. At that moment, the demon stuck its red wet muzzle into the tunnel and bared its teeth.

"There you are," it said. "My dear, dear Sister."

"It's *Mother* Superior," Mary Shelley said, thrusting the weapon forward and pulling the trigger. She had to admit a certain level of satisfaction at seeing the look of surprise on the demon's face before its head exploded in a splash of hot lead, black blood and gray bits of meaty chunks.

She pushed past the demon's reeking body and climbed out of the old waterslide. In the distance, a pair of red taillights flashed. Keane, leaving her behind. She couldn't blame him. For all he knew she was dead. He had to go after Anjelica. And it wasn't like he didn't know where Cadabra was taking her.

Calico Ghost Town was their next stop.

** ** **

Keane was impressed. He popped the last bite of his sandwich into his mouth, chewed and swallowed it, and then said, "Okay, so that explains what happened back at the Waterpark, but how'd you end up with that?" He nodded his head toward the side window of the restaurant where Mary Shelley's Sportster sat in the parking lot.

"Oh, that," Mary Shelley said coyly. "Well, I knew you were well on your way and it wasn't like you had a cellphone I could reach you on."

Keane nodded.

"So, I walked from the waterpark out to the freeway there. It's always busy, you know, people travel to and from Las Vegas at all hours. I got to the freeway, tucked away the MAC, of course, and just walked along the edge of the road, occasionally hitchhiking, most of the time just watching."

"And nobody wanted to pick up a tattered nun in the middle of the night."

"Would you?" Mary Shelley asked. "I mean, what are the odds I was even a real nun? I could have been a serial killer, or a pervert, or a prostitute who'd just been tossed from the vehicle of a man with a nun fantasy. I really don't blame anybody for not picking me up."

"But somebody did," Keane said.

"Yes," Mary Shelley said. "Somebody did."

** ** **

She had been walking along the side of the I-15 for about an hour. It was cold in the desert, but it could have been much colder. She was thankful for the thick material of her habit, not only for its warmth, but for the cover it provided to hide her machine gun. Dozens of cars, perhaps hundreds, had passed her and she had stuck out her thumb once in a while, hoping for a ride, but she was ignored most of the time and jeered at by others.

There had been a short period when no cars passed her going south, despite the north side of the freeway being nearly a parade of speeding vehicles, and that's when she first heard it. A low rumbling coming from a mile or so behind her, the classic *potato potato potato* sound of a Harley-Davidson motorcycle.

Multiplied many times.

It was a familiar sound that gave her surprising comfort and made her feel, strangely enough, *safe.*

She turned and looked up the freeway due north and saw their headlights. No doubt about it. It was a motorcycle gang coming her way. Whether it was an outlaw gang returning from a wild and crazy party in downtown Las Vegas or a group of weekend warriors on their way home after a week's worth of excessive drinking and accounting seminars, Mary Shelley couldn't tell from this distance.

But she knew this: This was her salvation coming toward her.

** ** **

"It was an outlaw gang, after all," Mary Shelley told Keane and Anjelica. She picked up the yellow wrapping paper from her breakfast sandwich and idly chewed the excess cheese off it. "Los Bastardos Unidos, out of Needles. And, unlike the hundreds of other so-called good Samaritans who had simply passed me by, they stopped to see if they could help a wandering nun in the middle of the night."

"Los Bastardos Unidos?" Anjelica said.

"Don't say that, honey," Mary Shelley admonished. "They gave me a ride to the nearest gas station where I convinced them to loan me one of their bikes to catch up with you two. I missed you in Calico but, boy, am I glad I caught up at Vasquez Rocks."

Keane was skeptical. "Wait just a second. They *loaned* you one of their bikes?" he said. "Lady, I've got a couple of problems with your story."

Mary Shelley gave him a challenging look.

"First," Keane said. "Why would any motorcycle gang just *loan* you one of their precious motorcycles?"

"Okay," Mary Shelley said. "I may have stretched the truth there."

"Ah-ha!"

"I didn't borrow it," she continued. "I bought it."

"You bought it?" said an incredulous Keane.

"There was about $40,000 in my go bag," Mary Shelley said. "I bought the Sportster for eighteen."

"What's a go bag?" Anjelica asked.

"It's like a little suitcase," Mary Shelley told her. "That's always packed so you're ready to go whenever you're ready to go." She patted her abdomen. "I keep mine here, on a belt."

Anjelica nodded. Mary Shelley could tell she thought that made perfect sense.

"Eighteen grand?" Keane said, shocked. To his 1954 brain, $18,000 was more than three year's salary.

"Oh, I overpaid," Mary Shelley admitted. "But I needed transportation."

"Okay," Keane acquiesced. "So, you bought it. But where the hell did you learn to *ride* it?"

Mary Shelley gave him a huge bright smile. "About five or six years ago we started a program," she said. "We contacted a local motorcycle club ..."

"Not a gang, but a club," Keane said. *West Side Story. 1961.*

"Yes, a club," Mary Shelley confirmed. "Because we wanted to reach out to the bikers and their families and try to get them interested in the church. One thing led to another, and the next thing I knew they had me on a bike." She tossed her hair and gave a nostalgic laugh. "We had a lot of fun and we actually rode with them quite a bit." She took a nimble sip of her Diet Pepsi and pointed a playful finger in Keane's face. "And that, mister, is how I learned how to ride a Harley."

Keane laughed. "That's some story, Reverend Mother." He drained his soda and tossed the empty cup on the table. "Well, we'd better hit the road," he said. He reached over and touched the back of her hand. "I'm glad you're back with us."

"Me, too," Anjelica added.

Mary Shelley gave them both a grateful smile and gathered up everyone's empty wrappers, greasy napkins and drained cups. She stacked them on the red plastic tray and stood, walking over to a nearby trashcan where she dumped the waste in the circular hole and stacked the tray on the little shelf built above it.

Keane held the door and they walked out of Tommy's. Anjelica automatically climbed into the passenger side of the Charger and Mary Shelley straddled the Harley, starting it up with a push of the button and giving Keane a big, wide smile.

Keane laughed as he climbed behind the wheel of the Charger.

"Nuns of Anarchy," he said.

CHAPTER TWENTY-EIGHT

"I can't *believe* this!" screeched the abrasive voice of Clay Watkins, supervisor with the dead jellyfish hair. "You screwed it up *again?*"

Grudgingly, Simon Cadabra allowed his eyes to peel slowly open. As expected, he found himself once again in the guest chair of Watkins' impressively dull office. Cadabra's head pounded with a monster headache that made the pain of being shot in the bridge of the nose seem tame by comparison.

"So, this time you really did it," Watkins went on. He jumped violently to his feet, slammed his palms down on the top of the gray desk and glared down at Cadabra with attempted menace. "And by did it, I mean you screwed the pooch. You had your chance, Cadabra. You were on your way out of here. You were *this close* to moving on. But, no. You blew it. You embarrassed yourself and you embarrassed all of us for having faith in you. We gave you every opportunity to put an end to a … to a *little girl*, for crying out loud … and you dropped the ball each and every time."

Cadabra closed his eyes again and wished for a quick, painless death. But he knew that wasn't in the cards. It was back to the cheating spouses circuit for him. Back to tempting people like poor old Dennis Harvey, who loved his wife with all of his heart but couldn't say no when someone with a smoking hot body like Lily Messerschmitt asked him if he was up for a quick game of hide the salami.

"What was your problem?" Watkins bellowed, spittle flying from his lips like shrapnel from an oil derrick explosion. "You had her right where you wanted her. All you had to do was pull the trigger and you wouldn't be here. *I* wouldn't be here. We both would have moved onto the next plane. But you weren't man enough to do the deed."

"Clay," said Cadabra evenly. "Do me a favor and shut the hell up, would ya? I've got a headache the size of Cincinnati."

"You think you've got a headache now, magic man?" Watkins shrieked. "Wait until The Boss gets here. Yeah, that's right. He's coming up and he's taking over. First, he's going to come in here and kick both of our asses, and then he's going to take over the mission himself."

"Good," said Cadabra. "Let him." He stood abruptly and stared down at Watkins, letting the two feet he had over his supervisor do its intimidation work. "I'm going back to my desk," Cadabra said. "If you need me, you know where to find me."

And he turned and walked out the door.

Behind him, he heard Watkins squealing in supervisorial fury. "You're not going anywhere! You're staying here with me! I'm not taking the heat for both of us!"

But Cadabra was already halfway back to his desk and had no intention of turning back.

CHAPTER TWENTY-NINE — June 6, 2015; 3:55am

With Mary Shelley and her Harley in the lead, they took Old Road up to the 126 onramp and merged onto highway 126, which would lead them through the smaller towns of Piru, Fillmore and Santa Paula before expanding into the larger town of Ventura. From Ventura, they would take the 101 to Santa Barbara and ultimately to the Old Santa Barbara Mission where Anjelica would finally be safe.

They drove past a sign with an arrow pointing off to the right of the main road that said "Lake Piru - 6" and Keane thought that sounded nice. What he wouldn't give for a weekend at the lake, a case of Sierra Nevada Pale Ale in the cooler, a fishing rod in one hand, his Kindle in the other. Maybe he'd re-read some Vonnegut, he thought, or finish up Robert E. Parker's *Spenser* series. *Or maybe I'd just nap*, he thought. *Lord knows I can use some sleep.*

He glanced down at the clock in the dashboard. It was just before 4:00am. Amazingly, he was just starting to feel the first real edges of true exhaustion. It had been a long day, and a hard one. His body and soul had taken quite a beating but he still felt awake and alert and, although he knew he was going to be sore as hell the next day, his limbs and muscles felt strong and ready.

He acknowledged that maybe the 44 ounces of Diet Pepsi he'd downed at Tommy Burgers had something to do with the alertness.

Keane looked down at the sleeping form of Anjelica on the passenger seat beside him. She was snuggled up in a little ball, rolled up tight like a dog sleeping in the cold, no doubt knocked out by the day she'd been through, not to mention the giant breakfast sandwich she had so eagerly wolfed down just a few minutes before.

The red taillight of Mary Shelley's Sportster floated in the darkness in front of the Charger. They were doing just five miles an hour over the posted speed limit of 60mph. Mary Shelley had told him she'd heard this was an especially dangerous road. It had been officially designated as the Korean War Veterans Memorial Highway, and Mary Shelley had joked that this was because more people had died in car accidents on this particular stretch of highway than during the entire Korean War.

It wasn't a particularly funny joke, Keane thought. But Mary Shelley had made her point.

The road had been divided a number of years back, with two lanes on each side now rather than just one, and the fatalities had diminished considerably. But there were still no streetlights here and, with the only illumination coming from the silvery moon, it was as dark as it could get at just before four in the morning. Keane felt somewhat uneasy driving in the near blackness and forced himself to concentrate on the road just a little more than usual.

There wasn't a lot of traffic due to the hour, of course, and before long Keane realized that the Harley and the Charger were the only vehicles on the road. Good. The lighter the traffic, the faster they would get to Santa Barbara and this would all be over.

As if on cue, a pair of distant headlights materialized in the rear-view mirror and Keane laughed softly. *Jinxed us*, he thought. *That'll teach me.* A moment later, a second pair joined the first.

Keane watched the headlights as they grew quickly, the vehicles behind him travelling at well over the speed limit, certainly more than the five miles an hour Keane allowed himself.

No wonder this is such a dangerous highway, Keane thought. *If people drive like that.* He could hear the first vehicle's powerful engine humming as it tore up the road behind him now and he steadied himself as it approached. Glancing at the side mirror, he saw that it was a large vehicle—a limousine or the like—and he wanted to give it a wide berth. If there was a drunk driver or a foolish street racer behind the wheel, Keane wanted to be ready to take the necessary evasive action.

In the rear-view mirror, he noticed the remaining two headlights separate and become two individual spots. *Those two are motorcycles*, Keane thought.

Instead of racing past him, however, the big car pulled up beside the Charger, slowed and matched its speed. Keane's eyebrows furrowed as alarm bells went off. What was this all about? He chanced a glance at Mary Shelley on the Harley in front of him but couldn't tell if she was aware of the new arrival or not.

Keane looked to his left at the car in the lane next to him and recognized it as a Lincoln Town Car, painted jet black, the moonlight reflecting off its obsessively waxed hood. The windows were tinted nearly black too, well past the point of being legal, Keane thought.

As Keane watched, the dark passenger side window of the Town Car slid down, its black glass revealing what looked like a red velvet interior, lighted in all the right places, giving the inside of the car the atmosphere of a lounge or ...

...*or a funeral home*, Keane thought.

He looked through the open window at the driver, expecting to see a drunken chauffeur or a wasted rich kid at the wheel. His breath caught in his throat as his eyes took in the heavy leather driving coat, the expensive leather-brimmed chauffeur's cap, the dark-lensed Ray Ban sunglasses ...

....and the bleached skull of the dead man driving it.

Keane stepped on the brakes, too hard, cursing when the harsh slowing jerked Anjelica into her seatbelt and yanked her out of her peaceful slumber. She gave out a little cry of surprise and fear.

He heard the Town Car's engine roar and his heart climbed into his throat as the dark vehicle suddenly accelerated, zipped past the Charger and clipped the rear end of Mary Shelley's Harley, sending the bike into a wobbling unsteadiness. Keane watched in horror as Mary Shelley struggled to keep the bike upright, couldn't control it, and sped wildly off the side of the road, through a wall of thick bushes and orange trees there, and then disappeared.

Before Keane realized what was happening, the Chauffeur's distraction had worked. With Keane's eyes locked on Mary Shelley's motorcycle, the driver in the Town Car ahead of him suddenly slammed on his brakes, bringing the Town Car to a sliding stop. Too late, Keane tried to veer around it but there was no time or space and the passenger side of the Charger scraped along the side of the Town Car, metal screeching and paint scuffing as the two cars abraded one another.

"Get on the floor!" Keane ordered Anjelica, as he stomped on the accelerator and felt the huge engine of the Charger kick in, rocketing the car forward. In his rear-view mirror, he saw the Town Car straighten itself out and start to give chase. Its rear tires billowed storm clouds of smoke as they bit into the road behind them.

And then the two single headlights, the motorcycles, roared past the Town Car on each side, bearing down quickly on the Charger. A moment later, they were on each side of it, matching the Charger's pace exactly.

Keane glanced at the motorcycle on his left and couldn't stifle a gasp. It was a Ducati 999; a bike Keane had heard described as a "crotch rocket." Atop the motorcycle sat a yellow-eyed demon, its thin forked tongue lolling out of its mouth like a foot-long racing ribbon, its eyes wide with mad blood lust.

A quick glance to the right gave Keane a virtual mirror image of the same thing.

There was no time for clever strategy. Keane whipped the Charger to the left, crashing into the first demon and then veered viciously to the right, colliding with the second. Both demons wobbled but didn't go down.

In the rear-view mirror, the headlights of the Town Car grew larger.

The Chauffeur was closing in. Keane was running out of time.

He couldn't outrun them, that much was clear. And he couldn't let the dead Chauffeur catch up before he dealt with the demons or the three-against-one odds would almost certainly be insurmountable. There weren't a lot of options.

Keane reached into his coat pocket and came out with a pair of driving gloves. He slipped them on, one after the other, and then rolled down the window on his side.

The demon on the driver's side took that as a sign. It revved the powerful 1000cc engine up to a screaming whine and pulled closer, its dagger teeth bared, its clawed hand reaching out for the Charger. Keane could smell its foul breath and hear its raw bacon-like tongue flapping in the wind.

Keane let it get close, closer. Just as the demon reached for the window, its filthy razor-sharp claws just an inch or so from the door handle, Keane's left hand struck out like a cobra and grabbed the demon's flapping tongue. He gave it a sharp pull and almost lost it due to the thick, slippery coating of sulfurous demon saliva. Gripping harder, he yanked the demon and its bike toward him. As the Ducati bounced first into then away from the side of the Charger, Keane felt a satisfying *snap* as the demon's tongue ripped out of its mouth, a spurt of black blood spouting out of the tattered nub left behind. The bike wobbled wildly and then flipped spastically, sending its driver over the handlebars and through the air like a dizzy superhero. The demon sailed through the air and then crashed head-first onto the pavement, its head bursting open like a spoiled melon.

Keane turned his attention to the second demon biker but was just in time to see that demon leap from its Ducati and onto the roof of the Charger. Keane stood on the brakes, heard a frightened whimper from Anjelica, and watched with satisfaction as the demon sailed overhead, landing on the highway just fifty feet in front of the Charger.

Keane mashed down the accelerator and the Charger roared forward, striking down the demon in a splash of red flesh and meaty chunks. The riderless Ducati wobbled to the right and smashed into the guardrail at the side of the road. It ran along the rail for a hundred feet or so and then coasted to a crooked stop.

Glancing into the rearview mirror, Keane saw that the Town Car was nearly upon him. He didn't like having the bony chauffeur behind him. It gave the other driver too much control. Keane never watched police pursuits on the TV in his office—he thought they were pointless and stupid—but he knew that a simple PIT maneuver could send the Charger hurtling into oncoming traffic or into the guard rail that separated the mountainside from the highway. So he waited until the Town Car had made up even more distance between them and then suddenly spun the steering wheel hard to the left, stamped on the brakes, and brought the Charger around 180 degrees, its tires squealing in protest. The Town Car raced past by them and Keane spun the wheel again, completing the 360, then punched the gas pedal and took pursuit.

Keane's victory was short-lived. No sooner had he felt the centrifugal force of the Charger picking up speed than he saw brake lights flash and the Town Car skidded diagonally across the road, blocking both west-bound lanes. Keane had to swerve violently to avoid t-boning the black car, and almost ran directly into an 18-wheeler coming the other way, its mighty horn blaring like a charging Tyrannosaurus Rex. Keane spun the wheel harder and the Charger skidded around in a half circle. Its rear fender slammed into the rear door of the Town Car with a crunch of metal and harsh metallic scrapes and then the Charger came to a complete stop, its powerful engine throbbing heavily even in idle.

If Anjelica wasn't in here with me, Keane thought, *I would have gone right through that bastard.*

In his sideview mirror, Keane saw the driver's window on the Town Car slide down, exposing the eerily lit red velvet interior inside. He saw a flash of the driver's bleached skull, and then a pair of dark cylinders eased out of the window.

Shotgun, Keane realized suddenly. *A goddamn big one.* Easily the size of the Simon Cadabra's. Maybe even bigger.

Keane ducked down behind the seat as the shotgun spat flame and the rear window of the Charger exploded into a million diamond-like pieces. *So that's how you want to play?* Keane thought.

He snatched the .45 out of the recess beside the driver's seat and pointed the weapon out the back window. His conversation with Buster of the day before (had it really been only the day before?) came back to him:

"It's your gun," Buster had told him. "But with one major modification: It will never run out of ammo. As long as you can pull the trigger, the gun will continue to fire."

So Keane pulled the trigger, over and over, the .45 spitting bullets almost like a machine gun. He watched with satisfaction as they took their toll, peppering the driver's side window and the surrounding door with quarter-sized holes, tearing the upholstery up in angry puffs and taking out some of the eerie light on the red velvet interior. Ten shots, then twenty. Keane kept firing. One well-placed shot blew the sunglasses off the exposed skull in the Town Car, another punched a hole in its lipless smile. The Chauffeur's shot gun, seemingly forgotten, finally fell out of the window and clattered to the cool pavement below.

Thirty shots, forty and Keane finally stopped pulling the trigger. His finger felt weak from the exertion. He watched the Town Car for a moment, saw no movement, and then chanced a glance down at Anjelica.

She sat on the floor beneath the glovebox, her knees pulled up to her chest, her hands over her ears, her eyes closed tight.

Good.

He looked up just in time to see the Town Car door pop open, and the skeletal driver step out onto the street. Keane pointed the .45 again but the driver had already bent down, out of sight, picking something up between the cars.

Keane knew what it was.

The shotgun.

"Stay down!" he barked at Anjelica. He slipped the Charger into Drive, the .45 still in his right hand, and punched it.

He hadn't gone six feet before he heard another horrific blast and buckshot cracked into the Charger, most of it pinging away harmlessly into the dead night air but a few pieces ricocheting around in the car's interior. Keane felt a piece whisk by his face and bury itself in the dashboard.

And then he heard a soft muffled cry and looked down at Anjelica. She was holding the meat of her arm near the bicep and a trickle of blood was snaking out from between her fingers.

She'd been hit.

Keane felt a hot rush of rage burn through him. He stomped down hard on the brakes, spun the wheel and negotiated a hairy U-turn that left the passenger side of the vehicle pressed up against the guard rail on the right and the driver's side facing the open road.

He stared hard across the road at the cadaverous chauffeur, who stood beside the Town Car with the shotgun broken open over his elbow. There wasn't enough of his face left to make any expressions, but Keane felt sure the Chauffeur was daring him to do something. Take some action.

"You okay?" Keane asked Anjelica, his eyes never moving away from the Chauffeur.

"Yeah," she said, unable to keep a whimper out of her voice.

"Let me see," Keane said.

Reluctantly, Anjelica removed her hand. Keane glanced down and saw a slippery red groove carved there.

"You'll be okay," he said. "It's gonna hurt, but it's nothing permanent."

He reached into his suit pocket and withdrew his handkerchief.

"Keep this on it till it stops bleeding," he said, opening the door on his side. "I'll be right back."

He stepped out of the Charger.

Standing in the middle of the road, its face half eaten away by .45 caliber bullets, the Chauffeur waited calmly beside the Town Car. As Keane climbed out of the Charger, the Chauffeur closed up his shotgun and held it down at his side. The battered remains of its skull stared blankly from the twin caverns of its eye sockets.

Keane's eyes narrowed. He raised the .45 and began walking toward the Town Car. He waited until the Chauffeur began to raise his weapon and then Keane began firing, pulling the trigger as fast and as often as his muscle memory would let him, aiming for the shot gun first, pelting it with slugs so that the Chauffeur couldn't lift it, much less point and shoot it. Finally, it tumbled out of the Chauffeur's hands.

Keane kept firing.

The Chauffeur took the hits casually, almost calmly. As if he knew they would do him no harm. When Keane had covered half the distance between the Charger and the Town Car, the Chauffeur began walking toward him.

Keane watched the Chauffeur approaching, the distance between them shrinking. He kept firing the .45, knowing full well now that it wasn't doing much good but taking pleasure in the fact that at least he was causing the Chauffeur some sort of discomfort, whether it was pain or just simple annoyance. Pieces of bone and shredded clothing flew off the Chauffeur as the bullets continued to hit their mark.

Keane didn't allow himself to think about what would happen when his path met the Chauffeur's. Didn't even stop to think that, if bullets weren't doing any harm, what good could his fists do? Instead, his mind was white hot with pure and unadulterated rage. He'd cross that bridge, and kill it, when he came to it.

There was thirty feet between them, then twenty. Keane kept firing the .45 over and over, taking pleasure in the pieces of bone and leather that his weapon was tearing off the Chauffeur. They both kept walking, like something out of a John Woo movie, Keane pulling the trigger over and over, the bullets taking their toll, the distance between them closing.

When they were no more than seven feet apart, Keane began to see that, despite the damage it was doing, the .45 wasn't putting the Chauffeur down. He focused on the white skull, putting hole after hole in the forehead and the cheeks, but still the Chauffeur came.

And then they were face to face and the Chauffeur slapped the .45 out of Keane's hand effortlessly, mid-shot, and it went skittering across the roadway. Before Keane knew what had happened, the Chauffeur reached out with its bony hands and grabbed him roughly by the throat. Instantly, Keane couldn't breathe. He grabbed at the chalky hands and tried to pull them away, but he was no match for the Chauffeur's supernatural strength. He struggled fruitlessly for a moment and then the world started to fade around him.

White spots danced before his eyes and he saw a glimmer of triumph in the blank gleaming skull. Keane had a last horrible thought as to what the Chauffeur would do to Anjelica if he didn't break free.

The thought didn't help. His mouth opened and closed, trying desperately to gulp some air. Multi-colored spots now swam before his eyes. He felt his legs give away and he crashed down onto his knees. He felt himself fading away.

The ground beneath him seemed to quake and a rushing roar filled Keane's ears. He was just passing into darkness when something huge *whooshed* past him and he saw a silver line of moonlight slash into the Chauffeur's throat and suddenly Keane could breathe, the cool air rushing into his grateful lungs. He watched in a daze as the Chauffeur's skull separated from its shoulders and soared into the air, tumbling there like a kicked football, and then fell to the pavement, shattering into a million dusty pieces.

Gasping for breath, Keane watched in grateful wonder as Mary Shelley turned the Harley around and headed back his way. She was riding one-handed, holding the Gorn sword high in her other hand, looking more than anything like Arwen in *The Lord of the Rings* movies that Keane loved so well.

His throat ragged, Keane slowly got to his feet, taking a moment to deliver a savage kick to the now motionless and headless body of the Chauffeur. Mary Shelley pulled the Sportster beside him and came to a stop.

"Bastard ran me off the road," she said.

"Saw that," Keane said hoarsely. He gave the body another vicious kick. "Guess he won't try that again."

"Anjelica okay?"

"She got hit," Keane said, and then, to Mary Shelley's alarmed look. "Just a scratch."

"Anybody else in there?" Mary Shelley asked, indicating the Town Car.

"Shit," Keane said. "Didn't think to look." He spun around quickly and yanked open the back door of the Town Car. The red-lit interior was empty.

"How far are we from Santa Barbara?" Mary Shelley asked.

"I'd guess about an hour," Keane replied. "If we hurry, we can make it by dawn."

"Let's hurry," Mary Shelley agreed.

She followed Keane to the Charger where he told Anjelica it was okay to get up off the floor. She took her place on the passenger seat and clicked on her seatbelt.

"You okay, honey?" Mary Shelley asked. She gently pulled away Keane's handkerchief, eyed the wound carefully, and then put the hankie back in place.

"Yes," Anjelica said quietly. "I am."

"Does it hurt?"

"A little."

Keane climbed in and started the car. "See you in Santa Barbara," he told Mary Shelley.

"Stay close," she said and spun the Sportster around and headed west on 126.

"How far away are we?" Anjelica asked, watching the Harley's taillights disappear into the darkness.

"About an hour," Keane told her. "Assuming we don't run into any more problems."

"Do you think we will?"

"I don't know," Keane told her. "I hope not."

"Me, too," Anjelica said.

Keane slipped the Charger into gear and pulled onto the roadway, settling behind Mary Shelley, and heading toward Santa Barbara.

Private Investigator Richard Keane had hoped that the drive to Santa Barbara would be uneventful, so he was happily surprised to discover that, so far, not only was it uneventful, it was downright pleasant. Anjelica had blessedly fallen asleep again in the seat beside him, and he was grateful that she was getting some much-needed rest.

The black, scabbing wound on her arm appeared to have stopped bleeding but it still filled Keane with an almost unbearable rage.

Keane drove through the sleepy town of Fillmore to Santa Paula, where the 126 transformed from a four-lane highway to a full-blown freeway. Following Mary Shelley's lead, he accelerated to 75 and drove without incident through the town of Ventura where the 126 merged into the 101.

Ventura was a town Keane knew well. He had often spent weekends there when he was alive, enjoying the small-town atmosphere and a particular bar there, The Sidecar, famous for its Singapore Slings. He wondered if the Sidecar was still around.

Of course, Ventura had changed dramatically in the nearly six decades since Keane had last visited. It wasn't such a small town anymore and was now crawling with streetlights, malls, and fast-food joints. Keane was pleased to see that the Ventura Pier still stood, reaching out into the moonlit water like a giant wooden arm, and that the cross on the top of the hill near the Avenue was still there, shining like a beacon and marking the town as its own. In the darkness, he couldn't make out whether the famous two trees were still located at the top of another mountain, but he hoped that they were.

He knew from past experience that once they reached Ventura Avenue, it was about thirty minutes to Santa Barbara and this was his favorite part of the drive. Edged by the mountainside on the right and the Pacific Ocean on the left, this had always been a pleasant drive which would take him past the tiny neighborhood of La Conchita (where Keane had learned that a tragic mudslide had occurred more than a decade before), the quaint town of Carpinteria and, finally, Santa Barbara.

Keane was looking forward to it. And kept his fingers crossed that there would be no further interruptions.

The moonlight sparkled like diamonds on the ocean on his left and the dark hillsides rolled by silently on the right. Keane was surprised and at first a little frightened when a towering flame suddenly rose up, lighting up the morning darkness on his right. When it did no harm, he guessed it had something to do with natural gas, a safety burn-off or something, and made a mental note to Google it when he got back to the office.

He drove past La Conchita just as the first rays of morning sun began to leak into the blackness of night. He couldn't see the wave of destruction from the landslide he'd read about that occurred there in 2005, and he was glad he couldn't. It had been a terrible disaster and he wasn't the type to gawk at the tragedy of others.

Even as more rays of sun seeped into the night, the road ahead seemed to darken just past La Conchita. Keane assumed it was because of the lack of streetlights along this particular stretch of highway, between here and Carpinteria.

He thought about what else lie between here and Santa Barbara and smiled at the memory of a restaurant that used to be just up ahead, with a giant DATE SHAKES sign that you could see clearly from the freeway and he wondered if perhaps it was still there.

Suddenly, Keane sensed that it was darker than it should have been. It took him only a second to realize he could no longer see the taillight of Mary Shelley's Sportster and alarm bells went off again for what seemed the *nth* time that day. He sat up straight in the Charger and stared forward into the darkness.

All he could see ahead of him was the road, the white lines that split the lanes shooting past him like short blasts from a ray gun. Even the moon's waning glow and the morning's dawning light failed to sparkle on the ocean to his left.

And then, suddenly, impossibly, there was somebody standing in the middle of the road and there was no way to avoid them. Keane stood on the brakes, but it was too late. The Charger slammed into the person and threw them onto the hood, their face pressed against the windshield.

Angelica gave out a little scream.

A moment later, Keane joined her.

Because the face on the windshield was a face they both knew. A red face, sporting a jet-black van-dyke beard, a face with yellow eyes and a sardonic smile pressed into its ruby lips.

A face that emitted an eerie red glow and sported two red horns just above its forehead.

Yep. It was The Boss.

Satan.

The lack of response time and the shock of the impact had sent the Charger slewing across the highway, its tires squealing across both lanes. Keane spun the wheel uselessly and the car slid off the pavement and onto the gravel roadside where its rear passenger side slammed into a telephone pole with a terrible crunching sound.

Keane shook his head to clear it, glanced over at Anjelica and was horrified to see she was covered in broken window glass, out like a light, her tiny forehead bleeding. He reached out to touch her, to make sure she was all right, when the man on the hood suddenly peeled himself away from the windshield, brushed off his blood red tuxedo (which Keane guessed was about two sizes too small for him) and stood in front of the Charger, his grim smile turning into a broad grin.

Keane saw that his teeth, like his eyes, were a sickly yellow, too.

Satan gave Keane a satisfied look and then came around to the driver side door. Keane fumbled for the .45 but it was jammed into its holster at an odd angle and he couldn't get a grip on it.

A red hand, its black fingernails hideously long and sharp but remarkably well-manicured, grabbed the door handle of the Charger and ripped the door away as though it were paper. Satan casually tossed it over his shoulder, where it crashed onto the pavement, its window glass instantly shattering into a million glittering pieces. Satan stared down at him.

"Mr. Keane," he said, his voice smooth, velvety and nails-on-chalkboard annoying all at once, "You have been a royal pain in my ass today."

The red hand grabbed at the seatbelt around Keane's waist and ripped it away, snapping it off as though it were a stale rubber band. Then the hand grabbed a fistful of Keane's suit jacket and yanked him out of the car, spilling him unceremoniously onto the street.

Pain flared up in every inch of his body as Keane hit the pavement. He felt the bite of every single pebble in the road as he tried, without success, to get to his feet. He fell back onto the road, staring up as Satan approached him.

The Boss' crimson tuxedo matched his skin color nearly perfectly. Beneath the two-small jacket, he wore a red vest, festooned with polished silvery skulls. The red trousers were about two inches too short at the bottom cuff but Keane realized that was probably to accommodate the pair of goat's hooves that protruded from them.

Satan's face was sharp and angular, not quite unhandsome but disturbing in some way because of its harsh nature. The sharply cut black beard was the only hair on the otherwise naked head. No hair on top, no eyebrows. The red horns on each side of the forehead looked as though they were actually beneath the skin, pushing up but not yet breaking through. A three-foot-long tail lashed out of the back of his trousers, its tip flaring into a perfect, fleshy arrowhead. The yellow eyes stared down at Keane with a curious but final determination.

"Do you know who I am, Mr. Keane?" he asked.

"I've got a pretty good idea," Keane said. "The flashy suit gave you away. What's that material? 100% baboon ass?"

Satan laughed without humor. "Good. You know who I am," he said. "So, who the hell are *you*? I mean, I know who you are and what you *were* but why did they choose you to bring the girl?"

Keane opted not to respond. He merely sat on the pavement in the darkness and stared up at those yellow eyes.

"You know, when they said they were sending a private dick, I thought, 'Great! This one will be easy.' But then you beat me at every turn." Satan laughed quietly. "Well, it's not exactly like I sent my best man," he said. "That damn magician is better at lighting himself on fire than following simple orders. But I thought, hey, why not? It's just a private dick. Even a washed-up Las Vegas magician should be able to handle this." He laughed again. "I guess I was wrong."

He reached into his jacket pocket and pulled out a long, thin cigar. "Mind if I smoke?" he said, adding quickly,

"Never mind. I don't care if you do or not." He scratched the tip of his finger against the side of his cheek and a tiny flame appeared on his fingertip. Satan lit his cigar, puffed it, enjoyed it.

"Nothing like a good smoke," he said. He puffed again, inhaled, held it. After a moment, he blew it back out, the smoke forming a perfect skull in the morning air before fading away into nothing.

"So, do you know what this is all about?" Satan asked. "Do you know why you were asked to protect this little girl?" He pointed a crooked finger toward the damaged Charger.

Again, Keane chose to remain silent.

"I asked you a QUESTION!" Satan bellowed, and his eyes turned black and his pointed tail thrashed, and Keane felt the ground beneath him tremble.

"No," Keane said. "I was told only that she was important."

"Ha! That's *rich!*" Satan said. "I wish I had more saps like you in my employ. Do what you're told without even asking why. Sheep, really. Hardly even people." He spat the last word with disgust, as though he'd found a hair on his tongue.

Satan took another drag of his cigar, blew out the smoke, which formed a billowy pentagram and faded to nothing seconds later.

"So, they told you she was important?" Satan asked. "But they didn't tell you why?"

Keane shook his head.

"That's because she's not," Satan laughed. "She's *not* important. She's just part of the game. The ongoing match between me and your ever-loving creator." He dropped his cigar to the ground and mashed it with one of his goat hooves. Keane was certain he heard the cigar cry out in pain.

"Do you like chess, Mr. Keane?" Satan asked him.

"Not really," Keane said. "I prefer poker."

"Of course, you do," Satan said. "But you are aware of the game of chess, no?"

"I am."

"That's good, because that's what you're in right now, Mr. Keane. You are in a big game of chess. The biggest game of chess in the entire universe. The game between good and evil, for lack of better words, for the prize that is the world."

Keane sat quietly, waiting for Satan to continue.

"You see, Mr. Keane, ever since the dawn of mankind, there has been a battle raging. But it's not really so much a battle as it is a game. A chess game, if you will. One side moves its pawn, the other side counters. Small battles are won but the game continues forever." Satan nudged Keane's knee with one of his hooves. Keane felt a wave of revulsion wash over him. "You, sir," Satan continued. "Are merely a pawn."

"I'm okay with that," Keane said.

"Yes, but the girl is only a pawn, too!' Satan cried. "Don't you see? Neither of you are important! Neither of you matter! You're just playthings and, whether I kill the girl or she gets to Santa Barbara, nothing will change! The game will go on."

"That's not my concern," Keane said. "My only concern is getting her to Santa Barbara safely."

"Yeah," Satan said. "And how's that working out for you?"

He stepped past Keane, his goat hooves clattering on the pavement, and walked around to the passenger side of the Charger.

Keane scrambled for the .45, unsnapped the leather strap there, unwedged it from its holster.

Satan ripped off the passenger door as easily as he had the driver's side, tossed it nonchalantly over his shoulder.

"You'll see," Satan said. "When she's dead, what will happen? Nothing. The world will go on. The game will continue."

Keane ran back the bolt on the .45, took something from his other pocket, something that glowed dimly in the darkness. He slipped it into the gun and rammed it closed. He forced himself to his feet and stood there unsteadily.

"Hey," he said, raising the .45 to firing position.

Satan looked up from the unconscious form of Anjelica to Keane, a look of curiosity turning into a look of amazement and amusement.

"Really, Mr. Keane?" Satan said, snickering. "Do you really think that your mortal weapons will have any effect on me? Do you really think you can kill *me?*"

Keane shook his head. "No," he said. "But I don't have to. I just have to buy myself some time."

And he pulled the trigger.

The Hell Shell spat out of the .45 with an explosion that rocked Keane back on his feet. It shot truly across the space between Keane and Satan, a fiery trail burning a line in the air behind it. Keane saw Satan's eyes open wide as he realized what was about to happen.

The Hell Shell caught Satan square in the throat, at just about Adam's Apple level, and buried itself there in the red flesh. A split-second later there was a fiery orange flash and a monumental POP!

And Satan was gone.

"Go to hell," Keane said.

Keane leapt into the Charger, turned the key and thanked God that the engine caught on the first try. He made sure that Anjelica was strapped in, was comforted by the fact that her flesh was neither deathly cold or feverishly hot, and pulled the Charger back onto the roadway.

The moment they hit the pavement, the dawning morning light returned and soon Keane was racing past Carpinteria, the Charger hitting speeds of over 90 mph. There was no more room for caution when it came to the police. When the devil was chasing you, a speeding ticket didn't seem so important.

Without doors, the wind gusts were cold and violent, but Keane ignored them. He didn't know how long it would take Satan to return from Hell, but he wasn't about to wait around to find out.

The Charger ripped up the 101, tearing past the few vehicles on the road as though they were standing still. Keane kept his eyes on the rear-view mirror, as well as the lane in front of him, constantly searching for any sign of Satan or his minions.

So far, the coast was clear.

He swung wide around a Volkswagen bus and cut off a BMW (its horn bleated angrily) as he pulled onto the Mission Street exit. He turned right on West Mission and a few minutes later turned left on Laguna. A second later, he saw it.

The Old Santa Barbara Mission rose proudly and regally out of the palm trees and vegetation of the land it was settled on. It was an astoundingly beautiful building, with its six Roman-like pillars, its centered round window, and the two double belltowers bookending the entire building.

Keane thought he had never seen anything so beautiful. That is, until he pulled up to the front of the building and saw Mary Shelley's Sportster parked in front.

The doors of the mission opened and about a dozen people, mostly nuns, spilled out of the building, led by a beaming Reverend Mother Mary Shelley. They surrounded the Charger, their joyous smiles balanced by their cautious eyes scanning the area for danger.

Something touched Keane's arm and he looked down to see Anjelica tapping him on the shoulder.

"Mr. Keane," she asked. "Where are we?"

Keane felt tears spring to his eyes. "We're there, Anjelica," he said. "We made it."

They took them in, they cleaned them up, they gave them food. Alone together in the massive dining room, Keane was enjoying a hot bowl of some kind of beef stew while Anjelica ate a bowl of Count Chocula cereal, the cartoon vampire on the front of the box looking a little too much like someone Keane had recently had a run-in with.

The door opened and Reverend Mother Mary Shelley came in. Anjelica was off her feet and had thrown her arms around the nun before the door even closed behind her. Mary Shelley pulled her close.

"I love you, too, honey," she said. "Now go finish your breakfast."

Anjelica ran back to her bowl and Mary Shelley took a seat beside Keane. "How you holding up?" she asked.

"I'm fine now," Keane said. "Mission accomplished and all that. But it was touch and go there for a while."

"What happened to you?" Mary Shelley asked. "I looked in the mirror and you were there one moment and gone the next."

"Yeah," Keane said. "We had a visitor." And he told her of his satanic encounter.

Mary Shelley's eyes widened in fear and wonderment as Keane told her his tale. When he was done, he took another spoonful of stew and watched as her mind tried to put it all together.

"So, it was ... *him*?" she asked.

"In the flesh," Keane said. "Thank God for the Hell Shell."

Mary Shelley looked over at Anjelica. "I wonder what was so important," she said quietly, nodding her head in the little girl's direction. "That he felt he had to come here to do it himself."

"I don't know," Keane said. "For a moment there, I thought he was going to tell me but, well, then the moment had passed."

The door opened and the Priest walked in. Father Austin Parker was a man of average build but stood only about five foot seven. What he lacked in height, he made up for with a take-charge personality that had endeared him to some of the churchgoers there and embittered others.

"Good morning, Mr. Keane," Parker said, stepping around Mary Shelley's chair and reaching across to shake Keane's hand.

"Good morning, Father," Keane said.

Parker continued around to Anjelica's seat. "And good morning to you, dear," Parker said to her, playfully ruffling her hair.

"Morning," Anjelica said, spooning in another mouthful of Count Chocula. Her eyes showed only slight annoyance at having her hair ruffled.

"Mr. Keane, I'm told we owe you a great deal," Father Parker said, taking a seat across from the detective.

"No reward necessary, Father."

"I was speaking metaphorically, of course," Parker said. "But we know what you've gone through to get the girl here and we want you to know we truly appreciate your efforts."

"I'm not sure that you do," Keane said.

"I'm sorry?" asked Parker.

"I mean, I'm sure you appreciate *our* efforts," Keane said, indicating Mary Shelley with an inclination of his head. "But you have no idea what we've gone through. You couldn't possibly. And you should be appreciative of that, too."

"Of course," Parker said. "I didn't mean to minimize what you've done."

"So, what happens now?" Keane asked.

"Well, we're going to take in Anjelica here as one of our own," Parker said. "She'll be safe here. No harm will befall her." He reached out suddenly, put his hands over Anjelica's ears, and whispered: "Not only do we have some of the best security in the world in our employ here, we also have one of the Church's largest armories." He removed his hands and got a surly look from Anjelica. "She will be safe," Parker continued. "And well cared for."

Keane nodded, satisfied. After all, this had been his assignment. To get the girl safely to Santa Barbara.

"Anyway, I just wanted to thank you two before you went on your way," Parker said. "I truly mean it when I say you may have saved the world."

"Wait …" Reverend Mother Mary Shelley said. "Wait just a minute. What do you mean, before we go on our way?"

"Well," Parker said. "I was told that you'd be returning to your convent in Las Vegas."

"And who told you that?" Mary Shelley said.

"I got an e-mail from the Vatican today," he said. "Saying those were the plans."

"Well, you need to e-mail them back right now," Mary Shelley said. "No, better yet, get them on the phone."

"But, Sister …"

"Don't you 'but, sister me,' Father. I've raised Anjelica like she was my own little girl. I've protected her for her entire life. I've *killed* for her. I don't expect to be pushed out of her life now. I *won't* be. So, you just get whoever sent you that e-mail on the phone right this very second and set things straight. I'm going wherever *she* goes, for the rest of my life. I'm not leaving her alone ever again. And we need to get that settled *now*."

"Very well," Parker said, and Keane could tell he realized there was no other option. "Come with me."

Parker and Mary Shelley left the room.

Keane looked over at Anjelica and winked.

"You go, girl," he said.

Private Investigator Richard Keane stood in front of the mirror in the Priest's room at the Old Santa Barbara Mission and admired his reflection. Sure, his suit was a little beat up and his fedora still had that damned hole in it (he had thought about getting it fixed one day and then realized he kind of liked it) but, overall, he looked pretty good. Trim, healthy, ruggedly handsome (if he did say so himself). *Not bad for someone who's officially ninety years old*, he thought, or *for someone who's been dead for fifty*.

He'd spent two days at the Old Santa Barbara Mission, most of those days sound asleep in bed or at the table enjoying the quite sumptuous meals they prepared for him, their hero. He felt rested now, and whole. And he'd seen enough of the daily procedures here to know that Anjelica was indeed in good hands.

He tugged at the edges of his suit jacket to smooth out the wrinkles and then reluctantly stepped away from the mirror. He took the stairs down to the main entrance and opened the double doors, enjoying the wash of sunlight that instantly warmed him.

He'd almost forgotten how much he loved Southern California weather.

There was a group of about twelve people waiting for him outside. They surrounded the remains of the Charger and, God bless them, they had done their best to fashion new doors out of cardboard for the war-torn vehicle. Keane knew they would no doubt blow off the moment he hit the freeway, but his heart glowed with the efforts of those who tried.

The first person to approach him was Father Parker, who reached out and took Keane's right hand in both of his. "We will never forget this, Mr. Keane," said Parker. "We can't thank you enough."

"Take care of her, Father," Keane said. "Or I'll come back for her again."

Parker laughed. "Don't worry, Mr. Keane," he said. "I assure you she'll be well cared for."

Keane looked over the Priest's shoulder to see Mary Shelley standing behind him, holding Anjelica's hand. "I know she will," he said. "I know she will."

He stepped past Father Parker and walked over to Reverend Mother Mary Shelley. She stuck out her hand and Keane ignored it, embracing her in his arms instead. A second later, she returned the embrace.

"Thank you for everything," he said into her ear. "I wouldn't be here now if it weren't for you."

"And *she* wouldn't be here if it weren't for you," Mary Shelley said. "Thank you for delivering her safely."

They broke the embrace and Keane knelt down beside Anjelica.

"Do you have to go, Mr. Keane?" she asked. "Do you?"

"I'm afraid I do," he said. "I'm going to miss you, Anjelica."

Tears formed in the little girl's eyes. Keane felt his own heart breaking. "Will you come visit?" Anjelica asked.

"I'll try," Keane said. "But that may not be possible."

Despite her attempts to be brave, a sob escaped Anjelica. "But what if I need you?"

"If you need me," Keane told her, knowing he was making a promise he was in no way sure he could keep. "I'll be there."

Anjelica nodded. A tear strolled down her right cheek. Keane gave her a quick kiss on the other side and stood, touching the top of her head (not ruffling her hair), and then stepping past her, to the Charger.

Keane stayed a moment, waving goodbye to the smiling faces of those around him. Most of them were unfamiliar. Some of them were new acquaintances. And some of them seemed like old friends even though he'd only known them for less than 72 hours. He waved one last time, peeled back the cardboard door, and climbed into the driver's seat.

"Very touching," said a familiar voice from the passenger side. "I almost teared up myself."

And then Satan reached into his coat pocket and withdrew one of those long thin cigars.

"Mind if I smoke?" he said. "Never mind. I don't care if you do or not."

Keane went numb. Just when it seemed like this was all over, here again was The Boss—Satan, Lucifer, Beelzebub, the Devil, the Beast, the Angel of the Bottomless Pit—sitting in the Charger with him, smoking a cigar that smelled vaguely like sulfur.

"What do you want?" Keane asked. "You can't hurt her now. She's safe here."

Satan seemed amused by Keane's concern. "You know something, you're right!" he said, lighting his cigar with a finger and puffing out a cloud in the form of an inverted cross. "She's safe here and, guess what, so are you! I have no power on hallowed ground. So, yes, she's safe, you're safe. For now."

"Then what do you want?" Keane asked again. He was aware that the people surrounding the Charger were still waving and smiling, not realizing what was going on inside.

"I just wanted you to know that your saving the girl means nothing," Satan said. "The game continues, as I told you. What you have accomplished today is utterly meaningless."

"Really?" Keane said. "And that's why you decided to get personally involved, because it's so meaningless."

Satan's yellow eyes seemed to flare a moment in anger. "And I wanted you to know that it's not over between us either, you and I," he said after a moment. "I don't take kindly to second place. I will make this even between us, Mr. Keane. I don't know where and I don't know when but one day I will have my revenge." He puffed again on his cigar, exhaled a cloud that formed a maliciously horned goat before fading away.

"Bring it on," Keane said steadily. "I'm ready when you are, Lucy. Now do me a favor and get the hell out of my car."

Satan, glaring, took one last puff of his cigar and vanished.

Keane sat quietly a moment, and then started the Charger. Despite the beating the car had taken over the past few days, her engine still roared with power. Keane decided he'd made the right choice when it came to choosing a vehicle.

He drove past the waving Mission people, paying special attention to Mary Shelley and Anjelica, and then drove out of the parking lot.

A few minutes later, he was back on the 101 freeway, headed South this time, relishing the golden afternoon sunlight dancing off the Pacific Ocean and the perfect 80-degree temperature.

The passenger side door blew off about ten minutes from the mission. Keane laughed.

As he drove toward Los Angeles, he noticed that the world seemed to be getting brighter. And brighter. And brighter. And soon he was driving into a white light that seemed to lead to nowhere and yet to everywhere.

The world disappeared around him.

Gary Leventhal sat at the counter of the Big Country Truck Stop Restaurant in Merkel, Texas and enjoyed another Diet Coke. The refills were free here at Big Country and Gary was never one to turn down a free beverage.

Using a piece of toast, he mopped up the last vestiges of gravy in the blue-rimmed plate on the counter and stuffed it in his mouth. Big Country had the best gravy in all of Texas, if you asked Gary, and when you put it on the top of a huge pile of mashed potatoes, Gary could think of no better meal.

Gary turned around and looked out the front window at his rig, which was parked just outside. It was a big Albertson's cargo hauler, and Gary was due to deliver its contents in about six hours, when the loaders arrived at the store to take the order. Now that he was done with dinner, he planned on going back out to the truck, lighting up his iPad and maybe browsing Facebook for a while, or maybe listening to one of the podcasts he followed on Spreaker: *The Friday Shot Day Show* or *The Backseat Mogul Show* maybe. Maybe he'd watch something on Netflix or even take a nap until it was time to meet his deadline.

Thank God for the iPad.

"Can I get my check here?" he asked the server behind the counter, a rather large woman named Dolly who Gary knew from previous visits.

"Sure thing, hon," Dolly said, as she had said so many times in her many years at Big Country.

Gary leaned back and let his meal settle a little. As he did so, he was surprised to see a woman step up to the counter beside him, and ask in a thick Texas drawl, "Is this seat available?"

"Sure," Gary said, looking up and down the counter at all the other available chairs. In fact, despite the fact there were several people sitting at booths, Gary was the only one at the counter.

"Thanks," said the woman. And Gary got his first real look at her.

She was about Gary's age, maybe a little younger, and she was *gorgeous*. Her blonde hair framed her face like a halo and her skin was smooth and vibrant. She had a small mouth that broke into a startlingly *huge* smile and she had a body that made Gary think of Bernadette Peters in her prime. She wore a white frilly dress that buttoned up the front and displayed just the right amount of cleavage.

Not bad.

"That your rig out there?" the woman asked.

"It is," Gary told her.

"Whatcha haulin'?"

"Um, groceries," Gary said, thinking that the four-foot-high letters painted across the side of the truck spelling *Albertson's* might have been a clue.

"Of course," said the woman. "Albertson's. How silly of me."

Dolly came over and the woman ordered a coffee. As Dolly went off to fetch it, the woman held out her hand.

"By the way," she said. "I'm Candy. Candy Johnson. You from around here?"

"Gary," Gary said, taking her hand. He was struck by the smoothness of her palm and the silky feel of her skin. "And, no, not from around here. Actually, from California. Just haul out here occasionally."

"Really?" Candy said, as if that was the most interesting thing in the world.

"Really," Gary confirmed, smiling, and, when Dolly returned with Candy's coffee, he ordered another Diet Coke. "How about you?" Gary asked. "You from around here?"

"Pretty much," Candy said. "Born and raised. I keep thinking I need to get away from here, you know, see more of the world, but I just can't get the time."

"I know the feeling," Gary said.

"So how long you on the road for?" Candy asked.

"I've got a few more runs out here," Gary said. "And then I'm heading back home. Been out on the road for about three months now."

"Married?"

"You bet," Gary said, flashing his wedding band. "Twenty years and counting."

"Must be a lovely woman," Candy said, the back of her hand accidentally brushing Gary's. "But don't you get lonely?"

"On the road?"

"Yeah."

"You do," Gary admitted. In fact, he thought, it's been a long time since I've even had a conversation with someone who wasn't involved in work. It was nice sitting here talking with this lovely woman.

"You know," Candy said, lowering her voice and leaning in closer to Gary. "I can help you a little with that loneliness." She waited until Gary looked her way and then casually popped the top button on her dress.

Despite himself, Gary realized he was aroused. "Um, thanks for the offer," he said. "But, as I said, I'm married." He flashed the wedding band again.

"Is your wife here?" Candy asked sweetly.

"Um, no," Gary said.

"So, she never needs to find out, does she?" Candy asked. Her hand snaked down to his knee, settled there a moment, and then traveled lightly up his thigh. "You like Candy, don't you?"

Gary felt his defenses melting away. "There is a sleeping cab in my truck," he said, and Candy's fingers tightened on his thigh.

And then, suddenly, a huge man seemed to appear out of nowhere. He forced his way between Gary and Candy, his girth pushing them at least a barstool apart.

"Okay, let's just nip this in the bud right here," said Simon Cadabra. "See, Gary, here's the thing: You're thinking she's out of your league and that you'll never get an opportunity like this again. And you know what, Gary? You're right. And there's a reason for that. And that reason is because you're being set up."

"Hey, asshole," said Candy angrily. "What do you think you're doing?"

"So, Gary, I'm going to ask you point blank," Cadabra continued, ignoring Candy's insult. "Do you want to take the chance of bringing home a case of the crabs to the missus …"

"I don't have the crabs!" Candy protested.

"Yes," Cadabra told her. "You do." He focused his attention back on Gary. "Do you really want to throw away two decades of marriage for three minutes of bliss? Or do you want to continue being the good guy and just step away from the counter, go out to your truck and drive away?"

Gary stared up at the big man in disbelief. After a moment, he dropped a twenty dollar bill on the counter, which was way too much for the Salisbury steak and mashed potatoes he'd ordered, popped on his Albertson's trucker hat, and wandered out to his truck. A moment later, the engine roared to life and the truck disappeared out of the parking lot.

"What the hell was that about?" Candy asked angrily. "Who do you think you are getting involved in my business?"

"Sorry, Candy," Cadabra said. "I just can't do this anymore."

"What am I supposed to do now?!" Candy asked. Then, abruptly, her tone softened. "So, what are you doin' tonight, sugar?"

Cadabra looked down, admired Candy's pouting lips and Betty Boop figure, and considered for a moment. Then, he smiled sadly. "Go home, Candy," he told her. "Close up shop for the evening, okay?"

And then he, too, walked out the door.

CHAPTER THIRTY-SEVEN

Richard Keane, Private Investigator, opened his eyes and found himself in total darkness.

Well, almost total darkness. There was a single circle of light beaming in on his cheek from the left. It didn't take him long to realize he was lying nearly flat on his back and his face was buried in the bowl of his fedora, the single shaft of light leaking in through the sixty-year-old bullet hole in its side.

He sat up, palmed the hat off his face and felt a wave of recognition wash over him.

He was back in his own chair. Back in his own office.

He was back home.

He was back Betwixt.

The blackness of space yawned out of the missing wall in front of him. Keane had always thought it mesmerizing and beautiful. Now, however, he thought it looked some-what empty and sterile.

He started to get up, to go grab a cold one now that his work was done, but then suddenly changed his mind, dropped back into the chair and reached for the cordless mouse and keyboard in front of him. The computer monitor winked on.

He navigated to Google.com and entered the phrase: "giant flame 101 freeway santa barbara." The first result to pop up, quicker than Keane expected, was headlined "La Conchita Flame: Question & Answer." He clicked on the link, read the data there and smiled.

"I knew it," he said aloud. "A natural gas safety valve."

He thumped his fist on the desk triumphantly, stood, removed his trench coat and hung it on the coat rack in the corner. Next, he propped his hat on the rack's topmost point. The bullet hole swung around and stared at him like an eyeless socket. *I should really have that repaired one day*, he thought, and immediately forgot about it.

He turned to go around the desk to the refrigerator and his eyes caught the giant TV on the wall. Did it look a little bigger than before or had he just been gone too long? He ignored it and stepped over to the fridge.

There was no doubt about the fridge. What had formerly been an icebox no bigger than two feet cubed (with a tiny, almost useless freezer drawer tucked inside) was now a dorm room-sized fridge with separate freezer and refrigerator compartments stacked one atop the other.

And now there was a small brown microwave oven sitting on top, too.

Upgrades, Keane thought. *I must have done something right.*

He pulled open the refrigerator door and was delighted, if not completely unsurprised, to find that his beer selection had been upgraded, too. Although there were still bottles of Sierra Nevada's Pale Ale inside, there was also a six pack of Stone's Arrogant Bastard ale. Keane took a bottle of the Stone, popped it open with the built-in bottle opener on the refrigerator door (*another upgrade!*) and went over to the absent wall.

He stared out at space while he slowly drank the beer, enjoying its rich heartiness and full flavor. There wasn't much to look at, really … nothing but blackness and glittering stars in the far, far distance ...but it was pleasant enough and there was always time for television and internet later.

He had almost finished the bottle when he heard a soft, wet *pop* and he knew instantly that it would be his old friend Buster the Cherub. He took a swig of his beer and turned to find Buster floating in the air near the absent door, the words 'Richard Keane, Private Investigator' hanging there in place as though the door were still there. Keane toasted the plump little cherub with a tip of the bottle.

"Evening, Buster," he said. "How's my favorite social worker?"

"Welcome back," Buster asked. "And, please, don't call me a social worker."

Keane responded by draining the Arrogant Bastard bottle and tossing the empty into the RECYCABLES box. He went to the fridge, grabbed another, and then fell into his seat behind the desk. Buster buzzed over on his impossibly tiny wings and settled on the guest chair in front of him.

"It seems they think things went well," Keane said, wiggling the bottle.

Buster smiled, made an "it was nothing" gesture with his right hand. "You earned it," he said. "Your 60" TV is now a 70", your internet connection is now faster, and your food and beverage choices have been expanded." He pointed at the Kindle on the desktop. "Even your Kindle has been upgraded."

Keane took another sip of Arrogant Bastard. "I noticed," he said. "Did it go well enough for you to finally tell me who killed Kimmy Mukasa?"

Buster shook his head sadly. "As I've told you before, even we don't know who was guilty of that cowardly act. But the investigation continues."

"Swell," Keane said. "And I couldn't help but notice that I still find myself here. Stuck Betwixt." He set the bottle on the desk and looked across its expanse into Buster's puffy little face. "What gives? Didn't I do what they asked me to?"

"You did," Buster agreed. "And you did it quite well. You delivered the girl to the mission in Santa Barbara and you made all of the necessary stops along the way. Well done. Very well done, indeed."

"What was with all those stops?" Keane asked. "Seemed like a waste of time to me."

"On the contrary, Richard, those stops were of the utmost importance," Buster said. His little wings buzzed, and he hovered over Keane's desk, picked up the remote control there and pressed it into Keane's hand. "Turn on the TV," he said.

"Is Howdy Doody on?" Keane asked.

"Turn on the TV," Buster repeated, unamused.

Keane did as asked.

A newscaster appeared on the big 70" screen. She was dressed sharply, her make-up perfect and her professionally coiffed hair-do not a strand out of place. Keane thought she was probably on the way up and knew it.

She was standing before a structure that Keane recognized and he realized they had caught her mid-report. An electronic ribbon at the bottom of the screen read "Baker: The Big Comeback."

"And so," the reporter said, "This little town that acts as a rest spot for millions of Las Vegas travelers, both those going to Vegas with big dreams and those coming home with empty pocket books, has returned with a vengeance. On the brink of bankruptcy only two years ago, the town has enjoyed a resurgence of popularity, thanks to the famous chain restaurants who have recently opened here, the unique local businesses—including the likes of "Alien Jerky"—and this: The World's Tallest Thermometer, once falling into a state of disrepair and now a shining beacon to draw in weary visitors for one last stop to or from Sin City."

"You did that," Buster said. "Well, actually *she* did. Anjelica. Just by being there."

"How?" Keane asked.

Buster nodded at the remote control. "Change the channel."

Keane hit Channel Up on the remote. It was another news story, this one on the Financial News Network, and the reporter in the obviously expensive blue suit was saying, "Thanks to the influx of cash from Japanese investors, it looks as though Lake Dolores will live again, perhaps not as a waterpark but as a training camp for troubled youths, led by former pro footballer Donny Bennett. Bennett, as you may remember, lost his son to a drug overdose several years ago, and has long vowed to do everything in his power to help others before they lose their lives, too. The Pro Football Players We Care Camp is scheduled to break ground in early 2016."

"She did that, too," Buster said and, for a second, Keane though he heard the little Cherub's voice break. "Change the channel," Buster said again.

Keane hit the Channel Up button again.

It was another news story but this one was video from a live remote. Keane immediately realized that some kind of emergency was underway. Fire engines and ambulances were grouped together near one end of the screen while news vans and police cars were at the other. The banner ribbon at the bottom of the screen read, "6-Year-Old Boy Found Alive in Abandoned Mine" An excited female reporter was standing near a black, yawning cavern where fire fighters were lifting a young, blonde-haired boy out of the pit beyond. "I can tell you now that little Jonathan Douglas is safe and sound," she said, gasping between breaths. "He apparently wandered into these abandoned mines almost two full days ago and was trapped inside a shallow shaft without food or water. Fortunately, passing hikers heard his cries and rescuers were called in. Although the rescue was often endangered due to the threat of new cave-ins, rescuers were able to retrieve the boy without injury to him or themselves. The folks in Calico Ghost Town are calling the rescue a miracle."

Keane felt his eyes widen in wonder. "Change the channel," Buster prompted, and Keane hit the button again.

Still another news story, this one with a reporter that Keane recognized but didn't really care for thanks to his pompous nature and arrogant reporting style. He was walking slowly through a valley of rock formations, formations that Keane recognized instantly. The reporter held his sport coat slung over his back with one hand and a microphone in the other. "Vasquez Rocks," said the reporter, "has appeared in dozens of hit television shows and movies. You might remember this particular rock from an episode of *Star Trek*, or this one from *Austin Powers: International Man of Mystery*. What you probably don't know about Vasquez Rocks is that they're slowly being destroyed by vandals. Vandals with spray paint cans."

The scene cut to pre-recorded footage of several areas of Vasquez Rocks, their perfectly natural beauty destroyed by huge graffiti images sporting gang slogans or nicknames. There was no other word for it than "ugly" and Keane felt his stomach turn in anger and disgust.

"But now there's hope for Vasquez Rocks with this group of volunteers," the reporter said, returning to the screen. Behind him were a dozen or so men and women, all wearing the same green t-shirt with a white logo that read "Defenders of Vasquez Rocks."

"The Defenders of Vasquez Rocks are a team of friends and neighbors who decided it was time to do something to protect and preserve the history of these well-known rock formations and to educate the world on their importance and, of course, their natural beauty. Their founder, Jose Ramirez of Agua Dulce, tells us ..."

313

And the scene cut to Ramirez, a short but determined looking young man, whose name was emblazoned across the electronic ribbon at the bottom of the screen. Ramirez stared defiantly into the camera "We're here to protect the rocks," he said. "We have a patrol on duty 24/7 and a direct line to the local Sheriffs if trouble arises. If someone does get by us and the park is vandalized, it'll be up to us to clean it up again. We're here for the long haul."

"And at no cost to the taxpayers?" asked the reporter.

"None at all," Ramirez said. "We are 100% volunteers. We're doing this because we want to. Because it needs to be done."

The reporter stared meaningfully at the camera. Before he could give his usual obnoxious sign-off, Keane turned the television off.

"So, you see," Buster said. "Those stops were important. She needed to visit each of those four locations. They needed her help."

"Then why only those four locations? Surely there are hundreds, probably thousands, of others."

Buster shrugged.

"Of course," Keane said, rolling his eyes. "Mysterious ways."

Buster shrugged again.

"I still don't understand," Keane said, sitting back in his chair. "I mean, what did Anjelica have to do with any of that? Wouldn't those things have happened anyway? She's just a little girl. What was the point? Why was it so important that I escort her to Santa Barbara?"

Buster seemed to bristle, and Keane was surprised at the rare show of emotion. "She's much more than just another little girl," Buster said. "She's going to change the world in ways that no one before her has ever done."

"How?" Keane demanded. "She's seven years old. What the hell can she do to change the world?"

Buster stared gravely across the desktop at him. "She's going to be the first female Pope," he said simply.

Keane felt his breath catch in his throat. He closed his eyes and shook his head silently. He was sure he must have misheard. "Say again?"

"I said that Anjelica's going to be the first female Pope," Buster repeated. "She's eventually going to be the leader of the Catholic Church."

"Wait, wait, wait a minute," Keane said, flustered. "*The Catholic Church?* You told me this was never about religion! No God, no Devil, no heaven, no hell. No Purgatory. Just The Lightness and The Darkness. Was all that bullshit? Is that what you're telling me?"

"I'm telling you she's going to be the first female Pope," Buster said. "Eventually. And her tenure will bring the *world* together. She will reach out to all religions—and all non-believers, too—and they will *listen*. Her leadership will give the world a lasting peace the likes of which has never been seen before."

Keane's mind was reeling. First, there was the idea of a female Pope! Absurd! It wasn't even dreamed of in his era and wasn't that much more likely today. Then there was the fact that this little girl was just seven years old. How could they possibly know who she'd be when she grew up? It was preposterous!

But he remembered his time with her, and thinking that she would be capable of great things. Was it true? Could she actually be so important that she could change the face of mankind forever?

"Wow," Richard Keane said. He sat for a moment and just let what Buster had told him ricochet around in his brain. After a few minutes, he managed to eke out another "Wow."

He got up in a daze, walked over to the refrigerator and grabbed another Arrogant Bastard. Popped it open on the fridge door.

"By the way," Keane said flippantly. "Satan's real. I met him. You can call him The Darkness or whatever you want to, but I met him and, trust me, Satan's a good name for him."

"I am aware," Buster said.

"He told me nothing would change," Keane continued. "That what I was doing didn't matter in the big scheme of things. He told me the girl didn't matter."

"Of course, he did," Buster said. "And The Darkness has always been best known for telling the truth."

Keane laughed. "There is that," he said.

He walked from the fridge over to the missing wall, sipping his beer, staring out at the stars, trying to make out The Big Dipper or The Little Dipper or any sized Dipper at all, but he saw nothing but a sprinkling of stars, like salt spilled on a black tablecloth.

"So why am I still here?" Keane asked softly. "If we accomplished all we set out to accomplish, why am I still here? Why haven't I moved on to the next plane?"

"That, my friend, is nobody's fault but your own," Buster said.

Keane looked over his shoulder at the Cherub in his guest chair. "How's that?" he asked.

"Because you promised her," Buster said. "You promised her that if she ever needed you, you'd be there for her."

"I meant it," Keane said.

"And that's why you're still here," Buster said. "Because you promised. If you moved on, you couldn't keep that promise." Buster smiled. "We're helping you keep your promise."

Keane thought about that for a moment and then nodded. "That's okay," he said. "I kinda like it here. I kinda got used to it over the years." He took a sip of beer. "And I want to keep my promise."

"And you've got the upgrades," Buster reminded him.

"Ah, yes, the upgrades," Keane mused. "70-inch TV. Faster Internet, craft beer." He held up the bottle of Arrogant Bastard in his hand. "You know the only thing I miss?" he said, a hint of nostalgia creeping into his voice.

"What's that?" Buster asked.

"Fast food," Keane said. "Man, I love fast food."

"Open the microwave," the Cherub told him, smiling.

Keane could already smell the savory aroma of Tommy's famous chili wafting from the oven.

If you don't see the Shack, Take it Back, Keane thought.

And there was the shack, printed in bright red ink, on the Original Tommy's Hamburgers to-go bag inside.

ABOUT THE AUTHOR

R. Scott Bolton lives in Ventura with his wife Shelley, his son Josh and his dogs, Leo, Zoey, and Pretzel. He hosts internet radio shows for fun and you can listen to them by visiting his internet radio station/podcast studio at www.RoughEdgeFM.com.

Scott loves to hear from readers and welcomes e-mails at rsb@rscottbolton.com.